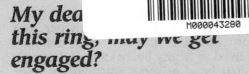

My dear... this ring, may we get engaged?

For a long while she simply stared at the ring. Then her hand hovered over it a couple of times, but each time she stopped herself from touching it.

How could she possibly be committing herself to Rob Stowe just by putting on his ring? Shouldn't he be the one to put it on, anyway—shouldn't he be there with her now?

And she suddenly saw the nature of her dilemma. She was still angry at being forced to play second fiddle to his business empire, and no ring, lovely as it was, was going to take away that hurt and anger. All of which, she told herself, is a recipe for disaster—another one....

LINDSAY ARMSTRONG was born in South Africa but now lives in Australia with her New Zealand-born husband and their five children. They have lived in nearly every state of Australia and tried their hand at some unusual, for them, occupations, such as farming and horse training—all grist to the mill for a writer! Lindsay started writing romances when their youngest child began school and she was left feeling at a loose end. She is still doing it and loving it.

Books by Lindsay Armstrong

HARLEQUIN PRESENTS®
1925—MARRIED FOR REAL
1986—ACCIDENTAL NANNY
2040—HE'S MY HUSBAND!
2057—HAVING HIS BABIES

Don't miss any of our special offers. Write to us at the following address for information on our newest releases.

Harlequin Reader Service
U.S.: 3010 Walden Ave., P.O. Box 1325, Buffalo, NY 14269
Canadian: P.O. Box 609, Fort Erie, Ont. L2A 5X3

LINDSAY ARMSTRONG

Marriage Ultimatum

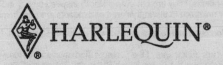

HARLEQUIN®

TORONTO • NEW YORK • LONDON
AMSTERDAM • PARIS • SYDNEY • HAMBURG
STOCKHOLM • ATHENS • TOKYO • MILAN • MADRID
PRAGUE • WARSAW • BUDAPEST • AUCKLAND

If you purchased this book without a cover you should be aware
that this book is stolen property. It was reported as "unsold and
destroyed" to the publisher, and neither the author nor the
publisher has received any payment for this "stripped book."

ISBN 0-373-12075-3

MARRIAGE ULTIMATUM

First North American Publication 2000.

Copyright © 1999 by Lindsay Armstrong.

All rights reserved. Except for use in any review, the reproduction or
utilization of this work in whole or in part in any form by any electronic,
mechanical or other means, now known or hereafter invented, including
xerography, photocopying and recording, or in any information storage
or retrieval system, is forbidden without the written permission of the
publisher, Harlequin Enterprises Limited, 225 Duncan Mill Road,
Don Mills, Ontario, Canada M3B 3K9.

All characters in this book have no existence outside the imagination of
the author and have no relation whatsoever to anyone bearing the same
name or names. They are not even distantly inspired by any individual
known or unknown to the author, and all incidents are pure invention.

This edition published by arrangement with Harlequin Books S.A.

® and TM are trademarks of the publisher. Trademarks indicated with
® are registered in the United States Patent and Trademark Office, the
Canadian Trade Marks Office and in other countries.

Visit us at www.romance.net

Printed in U.S.A.

CHAPTER ONE

ROB STOWE glanced out of his study window and whistled softly to himself. There was a woman walking up the pavement towards his house and, somewhat to his surprise, the mere sight of her filled him with spontaneous appreciation.

She was about five feet eight, he judged, in her twenties, with long dark hair and as she strode up the pavement, there was something about the way she walked that led him to speculate about her body beneath her coat. That long, fluid stride and her slim outline definitely seemed to suggest a lithe, beautiful figure, and the way she tossed her shining hair as she pulled something from her pocket, was more than enough to bring a smile of admiration to his lips.

Independent, he'd like to bet, as well as rather gorgeous, he thought, then stopped smiling as she stopped outside his house. Was this Brent Madison's replacement, he wondered, and swore beneath his breath.

It was three o'clock in the afternoon but the low, heavy clouds seemed to have robbed the streets of any colour and a chill wind was blowing.

Neve Williams pulled her long camel coat closer and glanced at the slip of paper she held in her gloved hand. This was it. An old but beautifully restored two-storied house in the fashionable inner Sydney suburb of Woollahra, it was the home of Rob

Stowe who, at the last minute, she'd been asked to interview for the magazine section of the paper she worked on.

Last minute wasn't quite accurate, she'd had a night and a morning to research her subject when her much more famous colleague had discovered he had glandular fever.

She hesitated briefly then opened the wrought-iron gate, stepped up two steps to the burgundy front door and pressed the bright brass bell.

There was a wait of about a minute as she shivered on the doorstep, and she was about to press again when the door opened to reveal a woman who was so attractive and so famous, Neve's jaw dropped and her eyes widened incredulously.

'Ah,' Molly Condren, star of film and television, said, 'you must be the person the newspaper was sending around in place of Brent Madison?'

Neve closed her mouth and thought swiftly. 'Yes. But not to interview you, Miss Condren, much to my great regret!'

Molly Condren smiled her famous three-cornered smile and tossed her equally famous red gold hair. 'That's sweet of you,' she said warmly, however. 'But you're going to have enough on your plate interviewing Rob. He's having second thoughts about it. Probably something to do with them having to send someone else—he knows Brent quite well, you see,' she added in an undertone. 'But come in! You must be freezing.'

The hallway was papered in chilli-bright red and lined with paintings. Molly indicated a rack and Neve hung her coat on it, ran her fingers through her loose, long dark hair and looked down at herself briefly. She wore a yellow polo-necked jumper tucked into caramel suede culottes, and long, polished brown boots. She picked up her capacious shoulder bag and prepared to follow Molly again.

But Molly was gazing at her thoughtfully. 'You look more like a model than a journalist,' she said with a faint frown. 'I don't think that will appeal to him, either.'

'Thank you! But looks can be deceiving, Miss Condren. Underneath I'm a journalist through and through and I'm quite used to dealing with—uh—difficult interviewees.'

'Oh, well,' Molly shrugged, 'just thought I'd warn you.'

'Warn her about what?' a deep and irritated voice said. 'For heaven's sake, bring her in, Molly.'

Molly surged through a doorway, saying, 'Darling, you of course! You may be Rob Stowe, the dynamo behind so many successful take-overs, but you're not in a very good mood today.'

Neve paused in the doorway and looked around. It was a large, lovely room, full of colour and there was a cheerful fire burning at one end. Sitting in front of the fire with his back turned to them was Rob Stowe. He was sitting in a wheelchair.

He made no effort to turn the chair and Molly looked heavenwards as she led Neve around it. 'This is the journalist who has come to do the interview you *agreed* to, Rob. And it's not her fault Brent got glandular fever,' she said pointedly.

'I'm well aware of that.'

'Good. Then I'll go and make some coffee.' She made a futile little gesture and left Neve to her fate.

But Neve had not been joking about her capacity

to do tough interviews and she looked into Rob Stowe's sardonic dark eyes calmly.

He was obviously a tall man despite being confined to a wheelchair, his thick dark hair was ruffled and touching the collar at the back of the football jumper he wore with blue jeans. His face was arresting.

It was a lean, angular face with lines beside the mouth and shadows beneath those damning dark eyes—marks of adversity and pain, borne and conquered. His mouth was hard, at the moment, but she'd seen photos of him laughing and the humour and vitality in his expression had been quite stunning.

Could she bring that humour and vitality back, she wondered, at the same time as she discovered herself to be determined not to make the first move, determined because he was taking his time about looking her over comprehensively.

She grimaced inwardly as his gaze rested squarely on her breasts beneath the fine yellow wool, before examining her trim waist at some length then her hips and the length of her legs. At the same time, however, she couldn't deny that a little frisson was running through her at this insolent, undressing-her-with-his-eyes inspection, and it both shocked her as well as annoyed her.

Shocked her because she wasn't used to men she didn't know having that effect on her and annoyed her sufficiently, she found, to toss her hair, put her hands on her hips and gaze coolly back at him.

'Well, well,' he said softly, 'you're rather arrogant, aren't you, Miss...I've forgotten your name?' He raised his eyebrows at her mockingly.

'Williams,' she replied. 'Neve Williams. No, not particularly, Mr. Stowe, but I don't really mind if you'd like to think so. And if *you* are having second thoughts about this interview, do please tell me and I'll take myself off.'

As she said this, an image of her editor swam through her mind and his last words to her printed themselves on her brain. *Don't come back without this interview, Neve. It's the first one he's given for two years so it's a real scoop.* Oh, well, she thought with a little shrug, what will be will be!

'What's that supposed to mean?' Rob Stowe inquired.

A faint smile curved her lips. 'I was just remembering that I could get fired if I don't get your interview, Mr. Stowe.'

'So what would you do if I did tell you take yourself off?' His sardonic gaze drifted over her again.

'I'd go. I don't grovel to anyone, sorry. Perhaps I am a touch arrogant,' she said humorously.

'Or are you a rather good psychologist, Miss Williams?' he suggested after a little pause.

'Perish the thought,' she murmured, but her eyes were dancing.

'Violet eyes,' he mused. 'I don't think I've ever seen true violet eyes before. Oh, well, you might as well sit down.'

'Thank you.' Neve sank onto a two-seater couch covered in fuschia pink linen, set at right angles to the wheelchair.

As she opened her shoulder bag, he added, 'Which is not to say you still won't have to front your editor without this interview.'

'I quite understand.' She took a pad, a pencil and

a small tape recorder out of her bag. 'You have no objection to me taping what you say, Mr. Stowe?'

'Provided I can edit the tape.'

Neve shot him a straight little look from her violet eyes. 'If you wish to, by all means. I believe the deal was that you would have the right to edit the whole interview?'

'Yes,' he agreed and looked at her thoughtfully. 'That doesn't upset you? It generally does upset journalists to have their often inaccurate version of things tampered with.'

'I look upon it as a challenge,' she replied coolly. 'A challenge to get things right to our mutual satisfaction.'

They gazed at each other for a long moment until he smiled slightly and said, 'One has to wonder what kind of challenges you like in bed, Miss Williams. With that figure I'm sure you'd be quite sought after in that—arena, but, let us begin.'

Don't respond, Neve warned herself. She did, however. 'One wonders whether you're capable of it, Mr. Stowe?'

To her amazement, he started to laugh. 'Got you,' he said softly. 'I knew you couldn't be as cool, calm and collected as all that. So few women are, especially when one resorts to the low, dreaded and chauvinistic sexual innuendo.'

Neve bit her lip. 'Could we consider ourselves square then, Mr. Stowe?'

'We could indeed, Miss Williams. How long it lasts is another matter. Where do you want to start?'

Neve looked around and tried to gather her thoughts. 'My editor suggested a bit of background although a lot of people know about you but we need to...' She paused and spread her hands. '—Interface how you've coped with this—an accident that left you a paraplegic who was told he may never walk again but beat the odds and will walk I believe— with the kind of man you are.'

'Coped? Very badly for the most part,' Rob Stowe said. 'As Molly will no doubt be able to testify. Won't you, Mol?' he added idly as Molly arrived with a tray.

'No I won't. You've been brilliant, Rob! You're an inspiration to many people. Don't let him deceive you!' she added to Neve.

'I only see two cups,' Rob observed somewhat dryly.

'I'm going to the hairdresser, darling. I'm also getting my nails done and my legs waxed. I should be gone for hours! But I'm sure you two will have plenty to talk about. 'Bye!' She waved her fingers.

'Bye,' Neve said quietly whilst Rob said nothing at all.

The pause lengthened until Neve said ruefully, 'I have a little formula, Mr. Stowe. What would *you* like to talk about?'

'You mean—anything?'

'Anything under the sun. And we can record it or not, it's up to you.'

He considered then smiled a little maliciously. 'Tell me about yourself, Neve. And you can record it or not as you see fit.'

'OK.' She didn't turn the tape on but she didn't look at all put out. 'I'm twenty-six. I was born in Western Queensland, on a sheep station. I did a Bachelor of Arts majoring in English at Queensland Uni and I was a cub reporter then parliamentary reporter for the *Courier Mail*. I came to Sydney three months ago, determined to escape politics for a while,' she looked wry, 'but didn't achieve it immediately. Until this break came up in the weekend magazine of the paper.'

'Mmm,' he said reflectively. 'I've read a couple of your in-depth interviews in the magazine. They were good.'

She looked surprised. 'Thanks. It's no hardship interviewing interesting people.'

A tinge of amusement lit his eyes. 'Married?'

'No. Nor engaged, nor in any way entangled at the moment,' she said.

'Why not?'

She lifted her shoulders. 'Too busy perhaps. How about you?'

'I should have thought the evidence of it was obvious.'

'If you mean Miss Condren—'

'Of course I mean Molly,' he said impatiently.

'Can I use that?'

'No.'

'Very well,' she said equitably. 'Is there anything else you'd like to know about me?'

'Yes. You should be on television. You look good enough, you can obviously handle yourself—ever thought of it?'

Neve smiled. 'Of course. But those jobs don't fall into one's lap. Besides, I like writing. I'd love to write a book one day.'

'What did your parents do?'

'My mother? Nothing much other than being a wife and a mother.' She paused and grimaced. 'But there were six of us so it was a full-time job. My father was the station mechanic.'

Rob Stowe sat forward and looked at her closely. 'So you've done well for yourself, Neve Williams? It's a fair haul from a sheep station to interviewing the rich and famous.'

'You did well for yourself, I believe,' she said steadily.

He looked quizzical. 'Are we two of a kind?'

She shook her head. 'I've got a long way to go before I get to your level of achievement.'

'All the same I feel we might be. Would you mind pouring the coffee?'

Neve rose. 'Not at all. How do you like yours?'

'Black with one sugar.'

She lifted her head and her eyes were dancing again. 'Then again, perhaps we are. That's how I like mine.' She placed a cup of coffee on the table beside him. But only a moment later, a large, excited, golden Labrador dog raced into the room and jumped up on her to bestow friendly greetings in the form of enthusiastic licks on her face, which she tried to avoid in a convulsive movement, but on top of the sheer surprise of the encounter, she only managed to trip.

The consequences were disastrous. She knocked over the table with the coffee cup on it, hot coffee gushed onto Rob Stowe who bellowed in pain, and she and the dog collapsed in a heap on the carpet.

At the same time a girl of about twelve with long red hair stood in the doorway with a hand to her mouth, and said mutedly, 'Oh, golly gosh!'

'Portia!' Rob thundered. 'Don't golly gosh me— it's the feeblest saying I've ever heard and how many

times have I told you not to let Oliver in! By the
way, I'm scalded! And—'

'Rob, I'm so sorry.' Portia rushed into the room
and on the way from the door, twitched a large linen
mat from beneath a bowl of flowers then applied it
to Rob wherever she could see any sign of liquid.
'As for golly gosh, the last time I swore, you threatened me with all sorts of unpleasant things so I'm
only trying to reform. Oliver! Will you get up! How
do you do?' she added charmingly to Neve. 'I do
hope he didn't hurt you!'

Neve sat up, observed the girl dressed in tartan
leggings, a forest green jumper and her red hair, and
she said a little shakily, 'You wouldn't be Portia
Condren, by any chance?' Then she felt her ankle
through her boot, and added, 'I'm sure he didn't
mean it but I may have sprained my ankle.'

'As a matter of fact I am Portia Condren,' the girl
replied. 'How clever of you but... Rob—' She turned
large dark eyes to him appealingly. 'What do I do
next?'

'Take her boot off—no, take the damn dog away
first. Then come straight back.'

'Yes, Rob.' She scampered off, dragging the un-
willing animal.

'Bloody hell,' he muttered and to Neve's consternation, started to lever himself out of the chair.

'Don't! Look, I'll be fine.'

But he took no notice of her and with the aid of
a crutch she hadn't noticed leaning against the chair,
swung himself upright then lowered himself carefully
to the floor beside her. The effort left him pale but
he immediately ran his hands up her boot, located
the zip and pulled it down.

He said, 'I'll pull the boot if you can, very gingerly, pull your foot.'

'I wish you hadn't—there was no need to get up,' she said anxiously. 'I—'

'Will you just shut up and do as you're told?' he said, but there was something curiously gentle in his eyes.

Neve swallowed, and between them they got her foot out of the boot. Beneath a yellow sock, her ankle was visibly swollen and when he pulled the sock off gently, it was also starting to go blue. When he touched it lightly, she flinched.

'It could be broken—*Portia!*' he called.

'I'm back, I'm back. Oh, g-goodness me!' Portia knelt on the floor beside them and eyed the ankle.

'That's as bad as golly gosh,' Rob said acidly.

'Well, what would you like me to say?' Portia returned offendedly and put a loving arm around Neve. 'You poor thing!'

'What I would like you to do, is ring the doctor. My mobile is in the chair.'

Portia jumped up and found his mobile. 'Your doctor?' she asked.

'Yes, but on second thoughts, give it to me and I'll do it.'

'No, I can. I know his mobile number is programmed in, in case of an emergency—'

'Look,' Neve said, 'if you could just call me a taxi, I can get to my own doctor, I'm sure it's not broken...'

But Portia was already talking excitedly into the phone. 'The thing is, Doctor Berry, by the way it's Portia here. No, no Rob is fine, well, he may be bit burnt but it's this lady, this lovely lady, and all because of me, Oliver knocked her over and we think she's broken her ankle. By the way, Rob is out of his chair and I *know* he shouldn't be—'

'Portia, give me that phone,' Rob Stowe ordered through his teeth.

But she ended the call, handed him the dead phone and said almost maternally, 'He's on his way.'

'What the hell happened to you?'

Neve leant her crutch against her editor's desk the next morning and sat down carefully. 'I sprained my ankle.'

'Oh. How did the interview go?'

Neve paused. 'It didn't.'

'Neve! I warned you. I also told you that he might be difficult—don't tell me you walked out on him!'

'George,' she said steadily, 'thank you for your concern about my ankle, but no, I did not walk out on him. I had almost to be carried out as a matter of fact—do you think that means I could claim worker's compensation?'

George Maitland blinked. 'You better tell me,' he said a shade uneasily.

'Well, I could have walked out on him. He certainly wasn't above using sexual innuendo to put me in my place, he gave me to understand he didn't think much of journalists and their often *inaccurate* versions of things and he asked me some very personal questions.'

'You didn't—you didn't get into a fight with him?' George said tentatively. 'I mean, I know you have your pride but a man in a wheelchair, Neve!'

'George, have you ever known me to get into a fight with anyone?' she asked ominously.

He shrugged. 'No. No, but I can't help knowing you're a mighty cool customer at times, Neve. That's why you're so good and you don't go around buttering people up, so, well, I just wondered if you provoked him into wanting to take a swing at you or something. You did say you had to be carried out!'

Neve dropped her face into her hands and started to laugh. 'Oh, golly gosh,' she said at last and looked into her editor's bemused face. 'No—here's what happened, George.'

'So it's still on?' George looked intent, even excited at the end of Neve's recital. She hadn't made any mention of Molly and had skated over Portia. 'I mean, you must have got closer to him during all this, even become friends!'

Neve looked away. At the same time someone knocked on the door and George called impatiently for them to come in. What emerged through the doorway first was a huge basket of flowers with his secretary staggering beneath it. She put the basket on the floor beside Neve and said laconically, 'For you.'

'Rob Stowe—want to bet?' George sat up eagerly. 'That would have set him back a couple of hundred bucks at least—roses, tulips, lilies, orchids and all out of a hothouse no doubt.'

Neve sighed inwardly and reached for the note pinned to the ribbon. Then her lips curved into a smile. 'As a matter of fact, it's from the dog.'

George's eyebrows shot up but he did say with a grin, 'And does the dog say anything about going back to finish the interview?'

'No, the dog does not. George, you have the most one-track mind I've ever encountered!' Neve protested.

George shrugged. 'Rather thought you suffered from that, too, Neve. So. Want to tell me why you've gone cold on the Stowe interview?' He eyed her narrowly and intuitively.

Neve sighed again.

'I mean, if it's only your ankle killing you or something like that, if it's only sprained, in a couple of days—'

'It's not that. I don't think he wants to do this interview, George.'

'But he agreed!'

'He might have, but I think he wishes he hadn't. And apparently he knows Brent so whereas he would have felt comfortable with him, I could be a different matter.'

'Neve, he's been giving interviews all his damn life, until the accident—look, do you know why he agreed in the first place? Because there was a strong chance he was going to be a paraplegic, that he'd never walk again, but against all the odds, he will and that's why he agreed. So other people confined to wheelchairs might get some inspiration.'

Neve was silent.

'Neve?'

'But did he actually suggest it or did you con him into it, George? Play on his finer feelings and so on?'

George blinked. 'This is an extremely tough businessman we're talking about, Neve.'

'He may not be quite so tough now.'

'Tough enough to set your back up before his dog knocked you over—look, there's only one way to resolve this.' He reached for the phone.

'Don't—' Neve started to say but he ignored her as he told his secretary to get Rob Stowe for him.

She formed her hands into a steeple and asked herself why she had gone cold on the interview as George had so astutely divined.

Her mind roamed back to the day before. The rest of the afternoon had become almost like a party. Rob's Doctor Berry had turned out to be a jovial giant and he'd helped Rob back into his chair before dealing with Neve's ankle swiftly and competently as well as giving her a couple of pain-killers. Portia had made fresh coffee, and they'd all sat around the fire chatting.

There was no doubting Portia Condren was a very bright child. She'd asked Neve lots of questions about her job, surprisingly intelligent questions, and told her that English was her favourite subject at school.

It had also become obvious to Neve that Rob Stowe was actually very fond of Portia Condren despite her capacity for causing chaos—they'd described another couple of hilarious debacles she and the dog Oliver had wrought—and that Portia hero-worshipped him in turn. There was also something about the girl's dark eyes that had raised a question mark in Neve's mind—was she actually his daughter?

Then Molly had come home and joined the party with her unique form of delicious liveliness... 'I can't turn my back on you two for a moment,' she'd said, 'without heaven alone knows what kind of disaster happening. I can't believe *this* though...'

She'd been opening a bottle of champagne as she'd said it, however, of which Portia was allowed half a glass and Doctor Berry told Neve she could have one glass but no more on top of her pain-killers, provided she went straight home to bed.

But the most unique part of it all had been Rob Stowe himself, Neve mused while George waited impatiently for his connection. That vitality and humour she'd seen in a newsprint picture had been all the more dynamic in the flesh—until, that was, he'd clearly tired and the lines of pain had become more deeply etched in his face.

They'd all seen it and Molly and Portia had drawn close to the chair while Doctor Berry had looked at him professionally and made a discreet sign.

Neve had immediately pulled her own mobile phone from her bag and ordered a taxi. They'd all farewelled her warmly and apologized yet again but as she'd left, assisted by the doctor, she'd looked back at the group they made by the fire, and swallowed suddenly.

How could you know a man for half an afternoon, especially after a rather disastrous start, she wondered, coming back to the present, and know it would only be dangerous to see him again?

'Rob? George Maitland, here,' George said into the phone. 'How are you, old son? Fine? That's great... Yes, she's fine, too, well, she's hobbling around on a crutch but it's only sprained so she tells me so... Yes, the flowers have just arrived, she says to thank you so much! They've brightened her day immensely!'

Neve raised her violet eyes to George and they were scathing.

George ignored her look. 'Thing is, Rob, we were wondering whether you want to go ahead and do the interview? Neve's not too sure about it now but

Brent could be off for months and I had it slotted in with another story about a girl jockey who broke her neck and is a quadriplegic at the moment but she's determined to walk again...'

There was about half a minute's silence during which George looked tense, then, 'You will? Great. Yep, Yep.' He wrote something down on a pad and after exchanging farewells, put the phone down and looked at Neve triumphantly.

'Friday morning, eleven o'clock—it's Tuesday now, he reckons you should be more mobile by then. I'll have to reschedule it for the following week but it's definitely a goer, Neve. By, the way, take the next few days off until Friday.'

'Did you have to tell him *I* wasn't too sure about it?'

'I only spoke the truth,' George said virtuously. 'But I know you can do this, Neve, and, just between you, me and the gatepost, probably a lot better than Brent. He's getting a bit hackneyed. It's also an important interview, Neve, it's not *trivia*— don't forget that.'

By Friday morning Neve was a lot more mobile. She could dispense with the crutch although she still walked with a slight limp and her ankle was still slightly swollen although nothing to what it had been.

All the same it meant wearing a pair of loose, soft flat shoes and the only pair she had were bright blue suede that she actually used as slippers although they didn't look like slippers. She sat on her bed and tried to work out what to wear with them. Eventually she chose a pair of blue jeans and a rather elegant, long line, pewter jumper.

She still looked ridiculous, she reflected, as she stared at herself in the mirror and asked herself why she had ever bought bright blue suede in the first place?

Because they'd been fun, they'd been comfortable and she'd been several years younger, she answered herself and sat down at her dressing table.

She'd washed her hair when she got up, and she decided to confine its full dark bounciness in a knot. It looked better, she thought, as she lowered her arms and studied her face. More serious and professional-looking despite the shoes. And on a sudden impulse, she removed her contact lenses and put her glasses on instead. Very professional, she thought, but sighed.

Because nothing could mask for long, the deep sense of unease she felt about the forthcoming encounter with Rob Stowe.

She glanced over at the table she used as a desk in the bedroom of her small, rented flat, and all the papers that littered it, and got up to walk to the window.

Although the flat was small, it was comfortable, nicely furnished and above all, had lovely views of Sydney Harbour. It wasn't the harbour she had on her mind as she stared at the view, it was the compulsion, during her time off, to do as much research as she could about Rob Stowe, to add to the store of information she'd found in the paper's archives and Brent's somewhat meagre notes.

It hadn't been difficult. His meteoric rise to fame had been well-documented. One of four children born to schoolteacher parents, his grasp of trade, commerce and the stock market had seen him buy his first company at the tender age of twenty-three.

And he'd turned a run-down clothing manufacturer into a national icon for Australian sportswear. He'd sold the company for millions and moved on—everything he'd touched had been the same story. But what had kept him in the public focus, had been two things. His adventurous nature for one.

He'd whitewater-rafted down terrifying rapids in the inflatable dinghy he was, at that time, manufacturing, wearing the sportswear he still promoted. He'd driven around Australia on a motorbike and fished crocodile-infested waters with the fishing rods he made. He'd ridden a horse in the Quilty, the National Championship endurance ride of a hundred-and-sixty kilometres in a day, on a saddle one of his companies had made.

So he not only had a flair for trade and commerce, but an outstanding skill for promotion. The other thing that had kept him in focus had been his philanthropy. Every year he sponsored a national competition with science and arts awards for children. He also sponsored sporting endeavours.

Then, two years ago, not as a result of any daring deed but a motor collision in which the other driver had been drunk, he'd received the injuries that had made it unlikely he would ever walk again. And he'd gone into obscurity.

But what frustrated Neve was that the more she dug, the more she realized that while Rob Stowe might have had a very high public profile in some respects, his private life was another matter. At thirty-six, if he'd ever married, there appeared to be no evidence of it. There was no gossip of affairs or relationships—nothing. Which was no small feat if he was living with Molly Condren and, just possibly, their daughter.

A very private man, she mused, still looking unseeingly at the view, then amended the thought—when he wants to be.

She glanced at her watch and decided it was time to call a taxi. But on the short trip to Woollahra, she was still preoccupied although on two fronts now. She was beginning to make a name for herself as a journalist because of her quiet ability to dig deep and present the essence of her subject, not just the outer shell. To find fascinating facets people had not known about. Usually this involved extensive research as well as the knack of asking the right questions.

She now saw that she'd gone to the first interview with Rob Stowe more under-prepared than she'd realized, not her fault in the circumstances, but she now *knew* she was asking for trouble if she did her job too well, because the man already fascinated her.

She sat up suddenly and asked herself irritably what she thought had come over her? She was not an impressionable girl, she didn't fall in love at the drop of a hat, she was a dedicated journalist, wasn't she? So why had she experienced that undeniable frisson when he'd looked her over as they'd first met?

It was a question she discovered she was afraid to answer.

This time the burgundy front door was opened by a grey-haired woman in a pale blue overall. She was the housekeeper she explained, and yes, Neve was expected but Mr. Stowe was all tied up just at the moment so would she mind waiting?

Neve said no, she wouldn't, and once again hung her camel coat up in the chilli-red hall. She was led into the same room and sat down in front of the fire on the same fuschia linen settee. A cup of coffee was presented and, twenty minutes after her arrival, the housekeeper came to get her and took her into a book-lined study with a view of the street.

Rob Stowe was in his chair behind the desk, and on a wall table behind him was an impressive array of computer-ware, fax machines and the like.

He had a navy blue ribbed jumper on with military-style patches, jeans again, and he said immediately, 'I'm sorry to have kept you waiting, Neve. How is the ankle?'

'Almost back to normal, thank you. I'm sorry about my blue suede shoes. They're comfortable, though.' What made her say it she had no idea, as Rob gestured for her to back a few paces so he could see the shoes over the desk, and a glint of amusement came to his dark eyes.

Then it came to her—she'd said it to change the cool businessman persona he'd adopted that was so different from how he'd been after the dog had knocked her over. Come to that even sardonic and irritated, she thought, even being insulting would be better than this blank, professional wall.

But perhaps she was being too sensitive? Perhaps he hadn't had time to take his mind off whatever had been tying him up. Why, she wondered though, did she have the feeling that wasn't the case?

'Very bright,' he said, 'and not quite what one

would expect of an up-and-coming, serious journalist
although, the rest of you does qualify.' He raised his
eyebrows at her glasses and pinned-up hair but his
look of amusement faded swiftly. 'Sit down, Neve.
If you wouldn't mind, I'd like to get this out of way
fairly quickly. There's all sorts of turmoil going on
in the business world with this Asian currency crisis.'

She hadn't been wrong, she told herself and sat
down, thinking quickly. 'We could start with that, if
you like.'

He raised an eyebrow. 'What do you mean?'

'Well—' she pulled her notepad, pencil and tape
recorder out of her bag '—what you think of the
causes and effects of this crisis, how it might affect
your business, for example.' She flicked her pad open
and picked up her pencil.

'You're not serious?' He looked at her with a
frown.

'Why not? It could be an even greater part of your
life now.'

'Neve,' he said with controlled patience, 'all I
want to do is give people struggling to walk again
some hope—not set myself up as a consultant on
international crises.'

'I'm not asking you to do that, but you must have
some theories on it and people would be interested,
as a background to the man.'

'My background is well documented.' He subjected her to a I-don't-tolerate-fools-gladly look.

Neve remained unruffled. 'Not all your background, Mr. Stowe. There seem to be some significant gaps.'

There was a short, tense silence.

'Look,' he said softly but with that impatience

barely masked now, 'heaven alone knows why I allowed myself to be conned into this in the first place, but if you think you're going to get the scoop others have tried to for years, and get it under the guise of a do-good kind of article, you're mistaken.'

'You mean, the details of your love life?' Neve replied coolly. 'I can't deny that would be a scoop, and would be powerfully interesting to a lot of readers—'

'Not to mention yourself.'

'I'll ignore that, Mr. Stowe,' she said steadily. 'Because I'm on record of offering you an alternative as a background to this article. Unless all you really want to put on public record is how you've suffered and how you've risen above it.'

She closed her eyes as soon as she closed her mouth, and waited for the explosion. Truth to tell, she couldn't believe she'd said it but then she'd known this man got to her, just not how much...

None came. When she opened her eyes, he was staring at her expressionlessly. But he said, 'There's a name for the likes of you. A scavenger just about sums it up.'

'And there's a name for you, Rob Stowe,' she said quietly. 'A name a lot of Australians respect and admire. But if you want to keep your private life private, that's fine with me. If this article is to have the maximum impact, however, we need to make it interesting to everyone. Not only para and quadriplegics but the rest of society so that they may be persuaded to help with the cause.'

CHAPTER TWO

'AH, SO we've now progressed to flattery—what is it?' he barked as someone tapped on the door.

His housekeeper put her head round it. 'Mr. Stowe,' she said diffidently, 'you've got visitors. They've come for lunch.'

'Lunch?' he repeated blankly. 'What are you talking about, Judy? I haven't invited anyone and it's not even lunchtime yet.'

Judy came fully into the room looking anxious. 'It was Miss Condren. She must have forgotten about it when she and Portia went up north. Apparently she told them to come at eleven-thirty and it's past that now.'

Rob Stowe swore. 'Who the hell are they?'

'Well, friends of yours, too,' Judy said soothingly, 'and I can whip up something quick smart—Mr. and Mrs. Fanshawe and Miss Toni Simpson.'

'And I suppose you told them I was in?' Rob said witheringly.

Judy drew herself up but he added immediately, 'Sorry, Jude, didn't mean that. Oh, well, you better come to lunch, Neve. Who knows what kind of interesting background material you might find?'

'Thank you very much but I'd rather not,' Neve said.

'Why not?'

She looked at him. 'I should have thought it was obvious.'

'No, not to me, it isn't,' he replied blandly. 'I've mucked up your morning, your schedule, whatever, so the least I can do is give you lunch. And if you're worried about your blue suede shoes, Bunny Fanshawe is the most uncoordinated dresser I've ever seen. That's five of us, Jude.' He transferred his dark gaze to his housekeeper. 'I would apologize for the inconvenience but I know how much you love whipping up culinary masterpieces at short notice.'

Judy withdrew having bestowed a fond smile upon her employer as well as telling him he shouldn't exaggerate.

Neve simply continued to look at him steadily.

He smiled slightly. 'Do you normally wear contact lenses or have you, in the space of three days, suffered a sudden downturn in your eyesight? They're still the most beautiful colour, I must tell—'

'Mr. Stowe, five minutes ago you called me a scavenger—'

'Which you refuted most eloquently, Miss Williams,' he murmured.

'All the same, you then started to accuse me of flattery yet now you expect me to want to have lunch with you—I find that a little incomprehensible.'

'I'm like that,' he said ingenuously. 'Subject to irrational mood swings, something to do with being in a wheelchair, no doubt, and you can use that if you want to,' he added humorously.

'The thing is, I'm *not* subject to irrational mood swings, Mr. Stowe, and I'm only here to do a job.'

'One that involves getting to know me rather well if you believe your own eloquence, Neve,' he pointed out with subtle satire.

She bit her lip. 'However—'

'Look, if you put your lovely hair up and wore your glasses in case I was tempted to make a pass at you, Neve, only a verbal pass of course,' he said with irony, 'I am also aware of the dangers of our getting to know each other better. So. Have lunch with us now, observe another side of me if you like—and let's hammer this interview out this afternoon and get it over and done with.'

Neve's eyes widened and a faint tinge of pink came to her cheeks.

'Good. I see we understand each other,' he said briskly, and started to wheel his chair round the desk. 'After you, Miss Williams.'

The table was round and set in a glassed-in conservatory at the back of the house with a grapevine and lemon trees in tubs, growing inside. The conservatory overlooked a lovely garden with a huge mango tree and a pool—the work, it crossed her mind to think, of an inspired landscape gardener.

On the table there were linen placemats and napkins in a bright yellow, green and white floral design, the china was white Rosenthal, the cutlery had clear yellow acrylic handles and the wine and water glasses were heavy and green-tinted.

The whole effect was stylish and bright despite the clear though wintry weather outside. The soup Judy served as the first course was pumpkin soup with sour cream swirled artfully through it and chopped parsley sprinkled on it.

The company was lively. Bill and Bunny Fanshawe were middle-aged, he owned an art gallery and she painted. He was plump and stocky with a rich laugh, whilst Bunny was tall, thin and intense,

and draped in an amazingly garish selection of flowing clothes with lots of jangling jewelry.

Antonia Simpson—'Call me Toni,' she'd said immediately to Neve—was, by her own description,
idle and very rich. She was also a very upmarket
blonde in her early thirties, she spoke with an affected accent, she was beautifully dressed and very
attractive.

They'd all laughed heartily at Molly's forgetful-
ness and accepted Neve into their midst with warmth
and interest. It was immediately obvious to Neve that
they were all very good friends of Rob Stowe's.

Unfortunately, it had taken Neve a while to re-
cover from their host's last remarks to her before
they'd left his study, so she'd been a little quiet during the pre-lunch aperitif session. She'd also been
conscious of Toni's blink of surprise at her blue
suede shoes.

But Rob had chosen to explain why she was wearing them and everyone had laughed again.

It was Toni who said, during the soup, 'So why
have you banished Molly and Portia up to
Queensland, Rob?'

'I haven't banished them at all. You know how
Molly hates this cold weather.'

'Poor thing,' Bunny said understandingly. 'She
was born in Townsville, you know. That gives you
thin blood, it's so hot up there.'

'Neve was born in Western Queensland as it happens,' Rob murmured. They were sitting next to each
other and he glanced at her as he spoke. 'Do you
think you have thin blood?'

'I don't enjoy the cold,' Neve replied, choosing to
ignore the double entendre which might just as well

have said, *You obviously have a thick skin.* 'But out west where we lived was a lot cooler than Townsville in the winter.'

'So you're *interviewing* Rob?' Toni frowned.

'Trying to,' Neve responded with a glimmer of a smile.

'First of all, Oliver had different ideas, then you lot descended on us,' Rob said as Judy cleared the soup plates. 'Bill, would you mind doing the honours with the wine?'

'But...' Toni paused. 'Do you really want to be interviewed, darling?' she said to Rob. 'I thought you'd—sort of—given all that away.'

'So did I. But Neve's editor—I'm sure you know how persuasive George Maitland can be when he sets his mind to it—twisted my arm in a manner of speaking. It's all to do with helping people walk again.' He stopped and grimaced. 'Supposedly, anyway.'

'It is,' Neve said quietly.

'I mean, I'm not sure I can say anything that will help,' he amended.

'Of course you can!' Bunny said bracingly. 'Don't you let him walk all over you, Neve,' she added.

'Now that,' Rob drawled, 'is something I doubt many would be able to do. She's *very* quick on the draw. And when do I walk all over people?' he asked injuredly.

'All the time,' his friends answered to a man, and they broke up laughing.

'As if you didn't know it,' Toni added languidly.

He shot her a wicked look but said to Neve, 'Perhaps you'd care to defend yourself, Miss Williams?'

Neve sipped some wine. 'Of the "quick on the draw" charge? Let me see,' she mused. 'I think it may have started when I was the only girl in the family with five brothers—'

'Five!' Bill blinked at her. 'You poor thing.'

'Well, it had its compensations. They were very protective—when they weren't teasing the life out of me. They were also responsible for me being able to ride, shoot, play rugby and do a lot of things most girls don't do.'

'And where are they all now?' Toni asked.

'All married and spread about the country,' Neve said. 'I was the youngest.'

'Do you *play* rugby?' Bunny asked wide-eyed.

Neve laughed. 'No, not now. But I have a fairly fair understanding of both codes.'

'Like to have a bet on the outcome of this State of Origin series?' Rob said lightly. The annual rugby league series of three games was played between Queensland and New South Wales with all the players irrespective of where they currently played and lived, reverting to play for the state of their origin.

'Of course. Queensland will win it.'

'Oh, now!' All the New South Welshmen at the table, comprising everyone else in the party, looked scandalized.

'I don't know why you're so surprised,' Neve said humorously. 'Queensland have already won one game.'

'And got trounced in the second!' Rob contributed.

'Neve, would you like to put your money where your mouth is?' Toni asked sweetly. 'I'm having a party next Friday night, the night of the final game. We're going to watch it on television, and I would personally like to bet you that Queensland doesn't win the series! Will you come?'

Neve hesitated. 'Uh—thank you so much but—'

'Oh, do come, Neve!' Bunny said intensely. 'Toni's State of Origin parties are such fun.'

'She's hesitating because she thinks she needs my permission,' Rob drawled as a little silence developed.

'What on earth for?'

Neve shot Rob Stowe a deadly little look from beneath her lashes, and said, before he could speak, 'Mr.—that is, Rob—doesn't want me to get too close to him. I'd like this interview to have some...new insights on the kind of person he is but he has, to put it mildly, some reservations about that. So, thank you very much, Toni, but in a sense, I'm persona non grata, really.'

'I've never heard of anything so ridiculous!' Bunny looked outraged. 'Rob, I've said it before and I'll say it again—there's no need for you to be a recluse.'

'Bunny, if there's one thing I reserve the right to, it's my privacy and I'm not a recluse.'

'Well, I agree,' Toni said.

Bill leant forward. 'But have you thought that you might have put Neve in a difficult position, Rob? If you agreed to it?'

'I didn't agree to Neve. Brent was going to do it then he got glandular fever.'

'If you ask me—' Bunny looked down her long, thin nose at him '—I wouldn't want the pap Brent has been turning out lately to have anything to do with me. No, I think you're on the wrong track, Rob dear, much as I love you. I think it will do you the world of good to get it all off your chest.'

'Bunny, much as I love *you*,' Rob said with a trace

of bleakness, 'don't tell me what I should and shouldn't do.'

'Oh, well.' Bunny shrugged and looked not in the slightest put out. 'Are you saying if Neve comes to the party, you won't?'

'I wouldn't be so juvenile. Well, Neve, another opportunity to observe the rich and famous—this time at play—has come your way,' he said maliciously.

'May I let you know, Toni?' Neve asked steadily and turned to Bunny. 'I'm sorry, you must think I'm quite dense, but I've just worked out that you're Albina Fanshawe and you were short-listed for the Archibald Prize last year.'

Bunny looked delighted and the conversation was safely steered towards portrait painting in general, and the Archibald Prize in particular during the next course.

By the time dessert was served it was two o'clock and when they'd finished, Rob said, 'Much as I'd love to linger over coffee with you, I'm afraid it's just not possible. Business calls—not to mention Neve and her interview.'

'Dear me,' Toni said. 'Chucked out, are we? Never mind, Bill and Bunny, I will shout you coffee. You do intend to give Neve some, I presume, Rob? You're not that much of a slave driver, are you?'

'Black and one sugar,' he said with a faint grin. 'Yes, I do intend for Neve to have some if she wants it, Toni. And I really don't think any of you need to worry on Neve's behalf, believe me, she can take care of herself.'

Judy brought a tray of coffee into the study not long afterwards.

Rob, who was on the phone, gestured for Neve to do the honours.

She poured two cups and pushed his over to the other side of the desk carefully. Then she sat back, staring at her own cup and trying to imagine how she was going to cope with the next assault.

He put the phone down, made some notes on a pad and threw his pen down. 'So.'

She looked up into his dark eyes. 'Are you sure you don't need to rest or something?' she asked.

'Quite sure,' he said briskly, 'but as a matter of interest, what makes you think so?'

'I, well, the other day, I saw that you got tired rather suddenly,' she said a trace awkwardly.

He waved a hand. 'I'd had a stint of physiotherapy before you arrived. Today is an off day.'

'Oh. Look, perhaps that's the opening we need,' she said slowly. 'Is it physiotherapy that's achieved the miracle of your being able to walk again eventually?'

'Hydrotherapy, physiotherapy, occupational therapy.' He waved a hand wearily. 'Therapy I'd never even heard of—plus a couple of titanium rods in my back.'

She blinked and made a note, then switched on the tape recorder. When he made no comment, she said, 'What about willpower?'

He shrugged.

'Did you, for example,' she persisted, 'vow to yourself that you would walk again?'

'I certainly didn't enjoy the prospect of a life in wheelchair but who would?'

'So you don't think your state of mind had anything to do with your recovery?'

'Neve, I'd like to take some of the credit, but the lion's share of it goes to medical science,' he said flatly.

'So—' she chewed the end of her pencil for a moment '—it's not also a question of willing yourself to stand the pain of endless exercises, a snail-like progress or what looks like no progress at all, the frustration of all the things you can't do, a drastically diminished quality of life, the operations—'

He held up a hand and said irritably, 'Of course it is. But there's still no magic password. Saying to yourself—*I will walk again*—is not going to do it alone—'

'But you did say that to yourself?' she interrupted quietly.

'Yes,' he said through his teeth. 'I said it, I shouted it, I cried it like a bloody baby, but if you really want to know what got me through apart from medical science, it was the people who wouldn't let me give up. The people who...lived through my rage and despair even when it was turned towards them, and never gave up hope themselves.'

'Medical people?'

'Some but also people like Bill and Bunny, Toni, Jude, my driver Jeff who's also a male nurse, and above all, Molly and Portia.'

Neve was silent for a moment. She looked around his study, absorbing on one level of her mind that it was a lovely room despite all the electronic hardware. The walls were panelled, there were a lot of books, the carpet was Persian and she saw that he was an admirer of the Heidelberg School of

Australian artists. A McCubbin and a Streeton hung on his walls.

She looked back at him steadily. 'Miss Condren mentioned the other day that you'd coped brilliantly.'

'"Miss Condren" has a conveniently short memory,' he said with irony.

'She also said you'd been an inspiration to so many. Would you tell me what she meant?'

He sighed suddenly. 'Each week I spend some time with people in similar circumstances, that's all.'

'All? I wish you'd told me this earlier.' Neve stared at him.

'What would that have achieved?'

'I mightn't have accused you of—some of the things I accused you of.' She blinked and took off her glasses. 'Then, we are united about one thing at least, I gather?'

'What would that be?'

'That this article could do some good.'

He picked up the pen, put it down and sipped his coffee. Then he said slowly, 'It's...let me put it this way, Neve. Yes, I hope it may, but one's own agony and how one copes with it, is not that easy to broadcast to the rest of the world. I would love to think that I was stoic and brave and manly and all the rest, but I know damn well there were times when I wasn't. And that's why I don't want to be represented as some hero type.' He lifted his shoulders.

'How would it be if I quoted you verbatim there?' she said after a short pause during which she'd thought deeply. 'And how would it be if I said, quite honestly,' her eyes danced for a moment, 'that I could *quite* believe there must have been times when you made everyone's life around you a misery?'

Nothing disturbed his expression for a long moment, then a glint of laughter came to his eyes. 'Give me an example.'

She tapped her pencil on her chin. 'Something like this—Rob Stowe, renowned entrepreneur and millionaire, is a handful, I have no doubt. I experienced his arrogance at first hand and it wasn't hard to believe his admission that during his convalescence, he made life exceedingly difficult for those around him...'

'Thank you,' he said, but with a trace of humour.

'It is all true, though,' she pointed out. 'Not just my inaccurate version of things.'

'I didn't think I was *that* arrogant.'

'If you'd been standing in my shoes you would have.'

He grimaced.

'Of course I'll go on to temper things,' she said seriously. 'So you don't come across as a complete monster.'

'Neve.' He watched her narrowly for a moment. 'I can tell when you're laughing at me despite your expression.'

'You can?' She looked at him innocently.

'Yes. Your eyes dance.'

It was her turn to grimace.

Before she could speak, however, he said, 'And how do you propose to rescue my image having thoroughly demolished me?'

'I can point to the loyalty of your friends, how good you are with children—Portia obviously adores you although I won't mention her by name. I can tell them how gentle and concerned you were with a wounded journalist.' She raised her eyebrows. 'I can…' she hesitated, then looked into his eyes. 'Tell them that I was moved by your honesty.'

He was silent.

Neve said after a long pause, 'And we can slant the rest of it towards how crucial the support you got from others, was.'

'All right,' he said abruptly. 'Go ahead.'

An hour later she switched the tape off and said humorously, 'I may not have lost my job after all.'

'George is being heavy-handed, I take it?'

'George—well, he has a job to do and that's to sell papers.'

Rob sat back and studied her. 'I would imagine things get quite lively between you and my old pal George Maitland, from time to time.'

'You could put it that way,' Neve responded with a grin.

'So when do I see the finished article?'

Neve thought for a moment. 'Monday probably. I'll work on it over the weekend, and then it will go into next weekend's magazine. Provided that you approve, of course.'

'Is that what you normally do on your weekends?'

She glanced at him. 'No. But this one happens to be free and my ankle could do with some more rest anyway.'

'So what do you normally do with your weekends, Neve Williams?' he asked idly.

'Go to the beach in summer, play tennis.' She shrugged. 'At this time of the year, take in a movie, a concert or an exhibition, do some housework, read, cook—all quite normal things, really.'

'I wasn't suggesting otherwise but do you do all this alone?'

'Not necessarily. I have some friends—'

'But no boyfriends.'

'No, I've told you that.'

Their gazes locked and she could see the curiosity in his eyes even before he said, 'I find that quite strange.'

'Join the club,' she murmured dryly.

He raised an eyebrow at her and said ruefully, 'Of men who find that quite strange about you?'

She merely nodded.

His lips twisted. 'I see. But you are attractive, intelligent and so on. Is it not rather natural to wonder why?'

She pursed her lips then said honestly, 'This is what gets me if you must know. What is so unnatural about being only twenty-six and happy and content despite having no man in one's life?'

He looked amused in a way that disturbed her for two reasons. The amusement was so like a man, she thought bitterly. Superior and quizzical as if she were a rare kind of bird indeed. On the other hand, even being all those things, he was undeniably attractive, vital and very masculine, damn him!

'Have there been any men in your life?' he asked then with a wryly raised eyebrow—a question that didn't improve her frame of mind.

'A couple,' she said evenly. 'Things didn't work out but I was also to blame. I am passionate about my career. I did see my mother virtually buried beneath children and housework and saw how hard it was for her so...' She broke off.

'You vowed not to let it happen to you,' he supplied.

'I certainly vowed to think twice before I got married and started a family.'

He was silent for a moment. 'Perhaps one of the reasons one wonders is because you sound very mature and you're obviously cool and clever but—that doesn't rule out a relationship,' he commented finally.

'Well, no, but the other thing you might like to know about me is that—' she grimaced '—shades of the country girl I once was and brought up to a very strict moral code, not to mention the way my brothers issued deep dark warnings about what men want, still linger in my psyche.'

He blinked. 'A bit of a puritan, Neve?'

'I'm afraid so.'

He frowned. 'But surely not still a virgin?'

She paused then her eyes began to dance. 'I'm only telling you this, Rob Stowe, because of the things you've told me that were, I know, not easy for you to say but—surely yes.'

'I'm speechless,' he said.

She smiled at him. 'Takes all kinds, I guess.'

'No, I didn't mean that. I'm full of admiration, to be honest.' His dark eyes rested on her thoughtfully. 'As to what I said before we went to lunch—'

'Ah,' she broke in, 'yes. I must admit you—surprised me.'

'I think we may have surprised each other, Neve, but it's the kind of thing that happens sometimes.'

'Not for me, in this context,' she said very quietly.

'Nor for me, but that doesn't stop it happening,' he responded a little impatiently.

She opened her bag and started to pack her things into it.

'Is that why you didn't want to come back?'

His question hung in the air for a moment or two.

Neve had replaced her glasses but she took them off again, rubbed her eyes and said briefly, 'Yes.'

'Despite being so arrogant and—unable to walk properly? Yet.'

'You weren't arrogant all the time.' She stood up. 'When do Molly and Portia get back?'

He laid his head back and drawled, 'If ever I've seen a case of covering up a left hook with a right jab, that was it.'

'If ever I've seen a ducking of the issue, *that* was it,' Neve countered.

'You're right.' He sat up looking amused. 'OK, shall we stop sparring?'

Neve blinked at him. 'By all means but—'

'Because I'm proposing to farewell you, Miss Williams, and get back to work. But in light of your feelings and my—commitments, perhaps it would be a good idea if our paths didn't cross again?' He stared at her, and his meaning was plain.

'I...' She swallowed. 'Yes, I agree, Mr. Stowe. Uh—they won't have to. Any amendments you'd like to make to the article you can do through George. I believe he's sending a photographer around, too, but I don't have to be here.'

'So.' He held his hand out across the desk. 'Like ships passing in the night, Neve, goodbye. Take care of your ankle.'

'I will,' she said, and looked at him fully for one brief moment. 'Take care of your back.'

It occurred to Rob Stowe as he watched Neve walk away down the street through his study window, that even when he'd been accusing her of being a scavenger, he'd been preoccupied enough with her not to notice Bill, Bunny and Toni arriving.

And a nerve flickered in his jawline as she turned the corner with that free, wonderful walk that was such an invitation to him to imagine her unclothed and in his arms...

He clenched his teeth, reached for the phone, and rang Townsville in North Queensland, to say, when he got through, 'For heaven's sake, Molly, when are you coming home!'

On Monday afternoon Neve sat in George Maitland's office again and waited tensely while George spoke on the phone. A copy of the article she'd written had been faxed to Rob Stowe that morning, and he and George were discussing it across the airwaves.

Finally, George, whom Neve thought had been unusually monosyllabic during the conversation so she had no idea whether he was getting approval or the otherwise, put the phone down and stared at Neve broodingly.

'He doesn't like it,' she said flatly. 'I warned you—'

'He likes it very much,' George broke in. 'He's given the go-ahead for it.'

'So why were you looking all doom and gloom?' Neve asked exasperatedly.

George's features creased and a twinkle came to his eye. 'Ever heard of the Walkley Award, Neve?'

'Of course I've heard of it. It's every journalist's dream to win one.'

'Well, I was pondering the fact that I may just have Walkley Award material in you. You did a damn good job with Rob Stowe—I wasn't sure whether he'd like you to be so honest about him but he said, "She got me, warts and all".'

Neve sat back but the usual glow of achievement didn't come. Only a slightly hollow feeling seemed to be inhabiting her. 'So, that's that,' she said.

'And nothing else came of it?' George inquired smoothly.

'Came of what?'

'Your encounter with Rob Stowe.' George said each word deliberately.

'No. What did you expect?'

George cocked his head and pursed his lips. 'You're a good-looking girl, Neve. He is not a married man.'

'He's a committed man, however,' Neve said before she could stop herself.

'I see. You mean Molly?' George waved a hand. 'They've known each other for years.'

'George.' Neve stared at him ominously. 'Do you mean to tell me you know a lot about Rob Stowe's private life?'

'Known *him* for years. Didn't think he'd want his private life exploited somehow, though. So Molly's still hanging around?'

'I…yes. No,' Neve contradicted herself. 'I mean, she's been a significant part of his recovery, so hanging around is hardly the way to put it.'

'Wondered if that's who you meant. I guess young Portia must be—ten now?'

'Twelve…'

'Oh, well, that explains it.'

'Is she…' Neve stopped herself sharply. 'I mean, she's a lovely kid. So. What's next on the agenda, George?'

George didn't reply immediately as he subjected Neve to a thoroughly unnerving scrutiny that seemed to see right through her. Then he said, 'A bit of fun.'

Neve raised her eyebrows but secretly breathed a sigh of relief.

'I don't know if you've heard of one, Antonia Simpson? Goes by the name of Toni, inherited a hell of a lot of money from her father as well as a lovely pad on the harbour and gives great parties. We've been invited to do a piece on one of her bashes.'

Neve could only stare at him speechlessly. As soon as she'd got home from Woollahra the previous Friday, she'd rung Toni Simpson and left a message on her answering machine to the effect that much as she greatly appreciated the invitation to the State of Origin party, she'd be unable to attend.

'Not…' She cleared her throat. 'Not the rugby league party?'

'Ah, so you've heard of it?' George said genially. 'By the way, she doesn't expect you to actually work all the time, she'd like you to do the piece from the perspective of a guest.'

'With a cameraman at my side? You—*someone* has got to be joking, George!'

'Neve, you know damn well that we try to balance the magazine so it's not too heavy—our readers love a bit of the social side of our high-fliers. You could make it humorous, you could—'

'This isn't exactly Walkley Award material we're talking here, George,' she broke in.

'You haven't got there yet, kid!'

'I didn't mean that.' She broke off frustratedly. 'That I'm above it or anything like that.'

'What did you mean?' he queried ingeniously.

'This kind of things is Brent's forte, not mine—'

'Don't I know it. Brent is the ultimate social climber, that's why he's so good on the party scene, but it may have escaped your notice that he is not here and we're all having to double up a bit.'

Neve frowned and opened her hands. 'How did this come about, though?'

'Rang me this morning out of the blue, she did. Suggested it herself. I told her that Brent had glandular fever which she already knew—you said something?' He eyed her as she muttered beneath her breath.

'It's nothing. Go on.'

'Which she already knew, but she said she'd met you and been impressed so why not send you along?'

'But it doesn't make sense!'

George raised his eyebrows and waited.

'Is there no one else you could send?'

'Neve.' He looked injured. 'I've said it before, but you *know* how shorthanded we are with Brent off.'

'I just hope Brent realizes what his glandular fever is responsible for,' she said sotto voce. 'So I have no choice?'

'In a word, Neve, no. And it will be a change for you. Something light-hearted and fun. Don't forget you've got Jason Stone, the Booker Prize man and the article you're researching on the rare stamp market. So far as the pics go, she's agreed to us only getting those people who want to be photographed as they arrive.'

* * *

To say that she was restless all week, was to put it mildly, Neve realized as Friday approached.

Restless and plagued by unanswerable questions. Should she ring Rob Stowe and tell him what had happened? Why had Toni, who'd appeared to agree with his desire for privacy, done this? Should she have just said no to George? What did one wear to a party, albeit one to celebrate rugby, at a harbourside mansion on the North Shore?

The only thing she'd sorted out in her mind by Friday afternoon was a decision on what to wear. A long, slim grey denim skirt that buttoned up the front, a violet blouse that matched her eyes and a silvery grey mohair vest over it.

Which was just as well because Friday afternoon was chaotic at work with the weekend magazine deadline zooming in, and it was a rush to get ready in time. And the traffic was horrendous and she was afraid she was going to be late. In fact she wasn't and she and the photographer received a gratifying number of approvals from guests willing to be seen in the social pages of the magazine.

Then the flow dried up, she breathed a sigh of relief because Rob Stowe had not been amongst the arriving guests, the photographer left and it was time for her to go to the party.

At the same time though, a big silver Range Rover drew up at the front door of Antonia Simpson's splendid house and the driver got out, opened the tailgate and drew out a folded-up wheelchair.

Neve was tempted for one unthinking moment to simply flee, then she steeled herself, and waited as Rob Stowe was helped out of the Range Rover and into his chair.

He didn't seem to notice her at first, she was on the other side of the vehicle, but as his driver pushed him round, he looked up and the sheer scorn that came to his expression was searingly visible.

CHAPTER THREE

'THIS is not what you think,' she heard herself say.

'No?' He looked up at her ironically. 'What do you think I'm thinking?'

'I...well, it wasn't my idea that our paths should cross again,' she said quietly.

'It wasn't? Forgive me, but I don't see any sign of force around—Jeff, could you ring the bell?' he said irritably to his driver. 'I *hate* loitering on door-steps.'

Jeff did as he was bid and Neve got annoyed. 'This is work actually, and for some reason or reasons unknown to me, Mr. Stowe, your friend Antonia asked for *me* to cover her party—were you aware she'd decided to get into the social pages?'

'I was not—ah, there you are, Toni!' he said as the door swung open and their hostess was revealed. 'What's this I hear about your going public with your State of Origin parties? If I'd known I wouldn't have come.'

'Darling, I'm sure Neve will leave you out of it if you prefer but I have a little cause of my own that I'd like to promote. But come in, come in!' She stood aside.

They all hesitated then at an abrupt gesture from Rob, Jeff the driver, got the chair up the steps and surrendered it to Neve. He then backed away towards the Range Rover murmuring that he'd be on call.

'Follow me, Neve,' Toni said graciously.

Neve hesitated again, and put her hands on the handles. But Rob Stowe said in a furious undertone, 'I can do it, leave me alone.'

'Of course,' she murmured shakily.

The hall and the passage they went down opened into a large veranda room with stunning views, a huge television screen set up at one end and about fifty people in it. And Rob was immediately besieged so that it was not difficult for Neve to move away.

It was a moment before she realized that Toni had followed her. Indeed she put her arm through Neve's and said charmingly, 'Let me get you a drink first, then I'll introduce you. I hope you don't mind me doing this, commandeering you so to speak—I gather Rob's not too thrilled about—something?'

'Me,' Neve said flatly

'Ah.' Toni was wearing the blue and white colours of New South Wales but in the very elegant form of a pale blue angora jumper over a long, flowing white skirt. She had pearls at her throat and in her ears and silver shoes on. She looked essentially chic and very monied. There were also blue and white ribbons and balloons festooned around the long table upon which a delicious supper was laid out.

'What is it between you two?' she added, scooping two glasses of champagne from a tray and handing Neve one.

Neve gazed silently across the room for a long moment. The fifty-odd revellers invited to this State of Origin party swirled, laughed and chatted, obviously in a festive mood and there were even a couple of people dressed in maroon, which told Neve she wasn't the only Queensland supporter amongst them.

She turned to the view of the harbour, fabulously

dressed in lights, and said, 'Nothing. Well, it was a difficult thing for Rob to do, the interview, and although we got it right in the end, I suppose he doesn't want a continual reminder of it.'

'You know, I changed my mind about that,' Toni said thoughtfully.

Neve blinked at her.

'Yes, I think Bunny was right,' Toni continued. 'He is in danger of becoming a recluse. Well, not exactly that so much, but he's got set in…certain ways. It seemed to me,' she added, looking Neve straight in the eye, 'that you might have the intelligence and the spunk to shake him out of himself.'

Neve shook her head slightly as if to clear her mind. Then she glanced pointedly over to where Rob's chair was surrounded although she could see through a gap in the throng that he was laughing and animated, and she said with irony, 'He certainly doesn't look too reclusive or set in his ways at the moment.'

Toni turned. 'When you know Rob as well as I do, you know what to look for,' she murmured.

'How well is that?' Neve asked after a pause began to grow between them.

'We were lovers once although in fact we were really only good friends. But he rescued me from a disastrous marriage, you see, and managed in that way,' Toni said softly, 'to give me back my self-esteem. For a while I wanted to wish it into more but he was always right when he said that what we were best at, was being there to pick up the pieces for each other.'

'Well…' Neve groped for something to say that would draw together the strands of the messages she thought she was getting but couldn't be sure. 'Molly is there for him now, surely?' She stared at Toni with deep uncertainty in her eyes.

'Of course. And Portia.' Toni smiled. 'All the same, don't take too much notice of his moods. Oh, there's Bill and Bunny! Come and say hello to them and I will get this party going.'

Bill and Bunny were delighted to see Neve although they were amongst the few who had declined to have their photos taken. They even commented on it humorously.

'How conniving of Toni!' Bunny enthused. 'She doesn't much like people interfering with her plans.'

Neve raised an inquiring eyebrow.

'Well, she obviously wanted you to come to this party,' Bill put in. 'So she got you here by hook or by crook.'

'She said something about a cause she wants to promote.'

But although Bill looked blank, Bunny looked oddly mysterious although she shrugged her shoulders and said, 'No idea what that might be. Now, Neve, who can we introduce you to? Let's start with...'

An hour later, the game was due to start, the delicious supper had been consumed and Neve had fended off several unattached men, and several women who had given her to understand they would be more than happy to feature in her article.

She'd just politely declined an offer from one such lady to visit her home and take in its wonders, perhaps even do an article on it, when a deep, sarcastic voice said at her elbow, 'You should have accepted.

Brent would have, he never misses an opportunity to social climb.'

Neve looked down into Rob Stowe's scathing dark eyes, and sighed suddenly. 'I really didn't want to do this,' she said quietly. 'I have no idea how *to* do it, come to that.'

'A bit of froth and bubble?' he suggested with deep satire and added, 'For heaven's sake, sit down. I loath being towered over, especially by women.'

Neve hesitated then sank onto a wicker chair next to him. At the same time a cheer went up as the kick-off whistle blew and the TV screen came alive with rugby league in all its glory.

'So George wouldn't take no for an answer again?' Rob said.

She nodded, her eyes following the game.

'Do you get the feeling we're being set up, Neve?' he asked then.

Although Queensland was approaching the try-line, her eyes jerked to his. 'What do you mean?' she whispered.

'I've got the feeling someone has decided you might be good for me. Someone who feels she owes me something. If not to say at least *three* people are in on it.'

Neve's eyes widened and her mouth fell open. He smiled maliciously and murmured, 'By the way, they scored. Queensland.'

Neve swallowed and looked at the screen but it was only a jumble of blue and maroon jerseys to her.

'I'm surprised at Bill, though,' Rob went on. 'He doesn't usually meddle in things he oughtn't to.'

'I don't think Bill knows anything—' Neve stopped abruptly.

'Ah, so the thought did occur to you?'

She licked her lips. 'Only just and I'm still, well, stunned by it,' she said barely audibly.

'Perhaps that's one thing we should have put into the interview,' he said dryly. 'How one's friends can also be a perfect menace when they think they know what's good for you and decide to gang up on you.'

'But...' Neve hesitated bewilderedly.

'You think they might have at least consulted you?' he suggested.

'Well, no, I hadn't got around to thinking that yet, but you have a point.'

'Should we—give them a run for their money?' he said with a suddenly wicked little sparkle in his eyes.

'How?'

'We could disappear—by the way, New South Wales have scored now.'

Once more Neve stared at the screen as the room erupted into delight. She shook her head frustratedly. 'I can't concentrate.'

'Does it mean so much to you?'

'No, it's only a game.' She shrugged.

'All right, let's separate inconspicuously, now's a good time for it, and I'll meet you at the front door in five minutes.'

'I...' She stopped helplessly then made herself go on. 'I don't think that would be a very good idea.'

'Possibly not,' he drawled. 'But there's nothing very much I can do to you, Neve, other than talk. Unless we've we talked ourselves out? Or you're re-pelled by this bloody chair?' And all the earlier anger—and frustration, she wondered suddenly—was back in his eyes.

'No—no, of course not,' she denied hastily. 'I mean—'

'Then I think you should just humour me for a while, Miss Williams,' he murmured dryly.

Ten minutes later, they were in the Range Rover being driven by Jeff to Woollahra. Neve, sitting alone in the back, felt like pinching herself. Another consideration was the deep feeling that she shouldn't be doing this.

But once inside the burgundy front door, another surprise came. Rob, having thanked Jeff courteously, levered himself out of the chair and with the aid of two crutches walked into the living room.

The fire was burning cheerfully, lamps were on and there was a covered tray on a warming trolley.

'Jude,' he said, stopping beside the trolley. 'She always leaves me a snack and a nightcap. What would you like?' He removed the cover.

There was a flask of coffee, two cups and a plate of sandwiches.

'Did Jude know I was coming?' Neve asked in a voice that didn't sound like her own.

He propped himself on his crutches and regarded her amusedly. 'Hardly. I didn't know myself that I'd be seeing you tonight. No, she always leaves enough in case I bring someone home. But if you'd rather have a brandy?' He raised an eyebrow at her.

'No, thanks. Coffee would be lovely.'

'Well, once again, would you care to do the honours? I'm going to do a few rounds of the room.' And he discarded the crutches, and did just that.

Neve watched for a moment, absorbing several things. That he was taller than she'd suspected, and lean with it. That each step was carefully taken with a look of intense concentration, and there was a dew of sweat on his temples as he passed her.

Then she drew her gaze away and poured two cups of coffee, selected a sandwich and sat down on the fuschia settee.

He circled the room six times then sat down carefully in an armchair. 'That should get the juices going,' he murmured, and laid his head back suddenly.

She waited for about a minute then got up and brought his cup over, putting it on a side table, and offered him a sandwich.

'Thanks.' He lifted his head, smiled at her and breathed deeply. 'Can't imagine why I went to Toni's party in the first place.'

'It doesn't...' Neve paused then started again, 'It doesn't seem to fit in with being a recluse.'

'I'm far from being a recluse actually, they just don't seem to realize it. But let's forget about me for a while. How has your week been?'

'Frantic.' She smiled faintly.

'Tell me.'

So she told him about the extra load of work she was carrying while Brent was off. Then the conversation became generalized. They talked politics and her time as a parliamentary reporter enabled her to contribute some funny anecdotes and some surprisingly mature views. They talked travel and she told him of some of the places she'd always wanted to visit and he told her about some of the more out of the way ones he had seen.

They were not for a moment lost for anything to talk about, sometimes teasingly, sometimes seriously, they laughed together—and when she finally looked at her watch, she was amazed to see that it was eleven o'clock.

They smiled at each other ruefully after her initial look of shock. He said, 'The game will be well and truly over.'

'I'll still back Queensland.'

'Would you like a nightcap now?'

'No, thank you. I should go.'

'It's Saturday tomorrow,' he pointed out.

'All the same—'

'Any plans for the weekend?' he interrupted.

'No.' She grimaced. 'You must think I'm a really dull person but this is definitely a housekeeping weekend. I'm so far behind it's not true what with all the extra work.'

'Does it take a lot to keep one single girl all house-kept, neat and tidy?' he asked idly.

Her eyes danced for a moment. 'You'd be surprised. There's washing, ironing—my oven is a disaster area! My shoes and bags need polishing, my hair and nails need attention.' She looked at her nails wryly.

'I can't see anything wrong with them. Or your hair.'

'But I can.'

'So you're a neat, fastidious person, Neve? Is that another side effect of being a country girl?'

She laid her head back and laughed. 'I don't know about that, but my mother was so delighted to have a girl after five boys, she drove me mad trying to keep me neat and sweet and feminine. Some of it obviously rubbed off.'

His dark gaze ranged over her and her eyes danced again. 'Don't say it,' she warned.

'How do you know what I was going to say?'

'Something in your expression told me that *sweet* wasn't exactly a description you'd apply to me.'

'You're right.' He looked amused. 'Far too clever for that, Neve Williams, although perhaps not as sophisticated as you appear on first impressions. Now, Molly, for example...' He paused. 'Is sweet but also sophisticated.'

Neve looked away, and came back to earth with a bump. 'When does she come home?'

'I don't know,' he said thoughtfully. 'We've had a slight disagreement.'

She turned back to him wide-eyed. 'So you did banish her to Queensland?'

'I've never banished anyone anywhere in my entire life,' he denied with a frown. 'Why the hell—'

'I wasn't the first to accuse you of it,' Neve said hastily.

'No.' The look he cast her was suddenly brooding. 'My dear friend Antonia Simpson was, if I rightly recall.'

'Look—' Neve went to stand up '—it's nothing to do with me and I wish I hadn't come, I shouldn't have—'

'There's no reason for you not to have come. It's my house and we've done nothing but talk.'

Neve sank back and to her utter consternation, she found her mind suddenly flooded with images of her and this man doing more than just talking.

And, as their gazes caught and held, she had the sudden conviction that his own words had opened the floodgates of his imagination. That it wasn't only she who was achingly conscious of a need to feel his hands on her breasts, it wasn't only she who was wondering what it would be like if they made love, slowly and gently, and fused not only their minds but their bodies...

She did stand up abruptly and she looked around the lovely room with a terrible sense of misgiving. 'All the same, I feel like an intruder, I feel as if I'm...' She shook her head.

'Poaching?' he suggested quietly.

'You brought Molly up,' she said defensively. 'You were the one who didn't want our paths to cross again—'

'And you were the one who made sure they did— no—' he gestured '—I'm not blaming you for what happened, but you could have warned me, Neve.'

'If only you knew how many times I picked up the phone,' she said with real distress in her voice. 'But each time I put it down because I said to myself, it *can't* be that real or that serious. I...even began to wonder whether I'd imagined it.'

'Sit down,' he said.

'If you don't mind, I'll just go,' she said hoarsely.

'Don't be a fool,' he replied sharply. 'You can't wander around on your own at this time of night, I'll get Jeff—'

'No, please.' She paused frustratedly. 'I'll ring for a cab to meet me at the corner.' And she left.

By late Saturday afternoon, due to a punishing bout of housework, her unit was sparkling, all her other chores were done, her nails manicured and her hair was washed and shining.

It was a wet, cold day and as she looked out of the window at the dusky gloom, she couldn't believe it when tears pricked her eyelids and a sense of deep loneliness overtook her.

How could the fabric of her life suddenly rip apart, she asked herself. Because of one man she was no longer happy and contented, no longer filled with a sense of achievement, no longer even at ease with herself. Instead, she mused painfully, she was filled with swirling emotions, strange longings and it was as if her centre of gravity had shifted slightly so that she might fall over if she wasn't careful.

A man already committed, she reminded herself. A man in a wheelchair, a man who could be diabolical when he chose but then again, painfully honest. A man, who, just to sit with and talk about nothing very much as they'd done last night, had made her...

What? she asked herself. Happy, just happy, she answered herself, but in a unique sort of way. With no tensions, no...was *that* it? she wondered suddenly. The absence of any physical tensions? She smiled painfully. Some very *physical* sensations but—perhaps no fears of being seduced willingly or unwillingly even, although she couldn't help thinking about it?

She put her hands over her eyes and wiped the dampness from beneath them, and shook her head. Useless to dwell on it, she told herself, so what to do? Work, that's it.

She turned up the reverse-cycle air-conditioning to cope with the growing chill, and because she felt sad, confused and bewildered, poured herself a glass of white wine and went to sit in front of her computer.

Yes, work, she thought savagely. Some froth and bubble in other words, to describe a party she should never have attended and had only seen half of anyway. And it suddenly struck her as pathetically ludicrous that she still didn't know the outcome of the game—she'd bought no paper, watched no television nor listened to the radio during her frantic day of housework.

Then the front doorbell rang. She frowned, picked up her glass of wine and went to answer it, which was to say, to open it with the chain still on and peer round it.

'Ah, a cautious girl,' Rob Stowe said. 'I know we didn't actually define the bet but since Queensland won and you backed them, I've brought us dinner.'

Neve blinked several times as she squinted round the door.

'You're not going to make me loiter on the doorstep are you, Neve?' he said plaintively.

'Uh…' She made a sound that was a mixture of bewilderment and exasperation and undid the chain. As the door swung open, Rob was revealed in his chair with Jeff behind him. On Rob's lap were several white boxes and in Jeff's hand, a wine cooler.

'Is that a yea or a nay, Miss Williams?' Rob asked gravely. 'I'm getting fairly warm in the lap area, in a manner of speaking—why the hell did I say that?' he asked himself gloomily.

A bubble of laughter rose in Neve's throat despite herself. 'I guess you better come in.'

Five minutes later, Jeff had departed, taking the chair, which Rob had exchanged for a pair of crutches. Rob was installed in an armchair and Neve was examining the contents of the boxes on the dining table. There was a homemade vegetable quiche, a cooked chicken, warm, brown and crisp in its foil wrapping, a dish of potatoes Anna, crusty rolls and a lemon meringue pie.

'Jude?' Neve asked, lifting her head at last.

'Jude,' he agreed. 'She said to tell you she is also a Queensland supporter—a scab in my own household!'

'I didn't even know they'd won.' Neve bit her lip as soon as she'd said it.

He looked at her consideringly. 'They won by two converted tries.'

Neve raised her glass wryly, 'Go the maroons! But...' She paused. 'How did you find me? I'm not listed in the telephone book.'

'George is.'

'George!'

'Don't blame him. I twisted his arm,' he said gravely.

'I'd like to believe that but I'm sure it didn't take much twisting. What did you tell him?'

He was stretched out in the chair and she registered that he was casually dressed in a tweed jacket, a round-necked navy T-shirt and jeans. She also registered that his dark eyes were faintly wicked as he said, 'Nothing, other than that I'd like to get in touch.'

'He'll be positively agog,' she murmured dismally.

'Just ignore him,' Rob advised.

'It's not that easy to ignore your boss—oh, well, would you like a drink?'

'Love one but I brought—'

'I've already opened a bottle of wine, it is a miserable wet Saturday,' she said ruefully, and picking up the boxes, made for the kitchen.

'What were you doing?' he asked a little later,

when she'd given him a glass of wine, closed the curtains and turned the lamps on.

She sat down opposite him. 'Trying to bend my reluctant mind to a bit of froth and bubble.'

His gaze drifted over her, taking in her shining hair, her neat oval nails painted with a barely pink enamel, her navy-blue track suit and pink socks and sand shoes. And he found himself wondering if she had any idea of how attractive she was. Had that strictly moral upbringing, despite her mother's attempts to render her sweet, neat and feminine, gained enough of a hold so she simply didn't set much store by her looks?

Or was she seriously serious by nature? Yet the way her lovely violet eyes danced at times didn't go with being serious all the time. And her figure, even beneath a track suit, was good enough to tempt most men. Me included, he thought dryly.

'Perhaps I could help, always wanted to try my hand at journalism,' he said, and grimaced inwardly because of how abrupt it had sounded. 'Uh—let's see.' He paused and thought for a good minute. Then he said, 'I have absolutely no ideas!'

He stared at her, so thoroughly surprised at his lack of creative talent, Neve could only start to laugh.

'Don't worry about it,' she advised.

'But I do,' he insisted. 'It can't be that hard!'

'Hard enough for me to have to look through some back copies to see how it's done. I could always start with Toni,' she mused. 'A New South Wales representative in pale blue angora, white silk and pearls. You know, I thought the upper classes, in Australia anyway, preferred Rugby Union? It is a private school, university sport here.'

'That's a rather damning assessment but, not that you'd know it, Toni doesn't hale from the upper classes. Her father was a fishmonger who had the nous to start a frozen food empire.'

Neve nearly choked on a sip of wine.

'Yes, it's amazing, isn't it?' he agreed humorously. 'The only sign of it that you'd ever see, is an absolute aversion to fish and the fact that when she gets really upset, she can swear like a fishwife.'

'So...so how did she get so...so...'

'Polished? Finishing school. And—' he looked cold suddenly '—marriage to an absolute upper class bastard who tried to dominate her by continually reminding her of her origins.'

Neve gazed at him wide-eyed. 'She told me how you—helped her to get over it.'

He looked surprised. 'Why would she do that?

Neve swallowed. 'I don't really know—'

'Come on, Neve.' He looked impatient.

'She,' Neve sighed, 'thinks I might be good for you.'

'So it *was* all a set-up! To get us together?'

'Well, I did decline her invitation but I imagine I will still have to do the piece,' Neve said dryly.

'Let's not split hairs.' He raised a sardonic eyebrow.

Neve studied the glass in her hand then she lifted her eyes to his and there was a trace of bewilderment in them. 'You told me you were committed. But you've done this—' she gestured towards the kitchen '—and last night,' she said helplessly.

He looked at her bleakly for a long moment. 'I thought the least I could do is explain things to you.

That's why I brought the subject of Molly up last night.'

'Should—' Her voice seemed to want to stick in her throat. 'Should we eat while you do it?'

'Neve…'

'No,' she said huskily and stood up. 'I'll be fine in a moment. Would you like to eat there or at the table?'

'I'm sure I can manage the table.'

'Good. Won't be long. I'll turn the television on for you.'

They were halfway through the meal before she said, 'OK—but can I just say this?'

'Be my guest.'

'Before you came this afternoon, I was really down in the dumps. I-it's the first time since I came to Sydney that I've felt lonely and not sure I was on the right track.'

He twirled his wineglass and frowned at her. 'What do you mean?'

'Well…' She paused and looked around. Although it was a furnished unit, she'd added some personal touches to it. A bookcase that was already threatening to overflow. Framed photos of all her family, a few lovely pottery jars grouped together with a variety of dried grasses in them. And on the table between them, her own colourful dinner service with a big floral design, set on rush placemats.

She started again. 'It's all given me a great sense of achievement. My job, being able to afford a nice place, the feeling that I'm in the centre of things and by that I mean news, culture, excitement—as opposed to a sheep station.'

'But this afternoon you felt different?'

'Yes, and I guess it comes down to having no one to share it with. It's never bothered me before. Our house at home was so crowded it was hard to have any privacy, then when I went to uni it was a hostel and even when I started work, I shared an old house with four other girls.'

She hesitated then went on, less positively. 'Of course, it's not that I suddenly want to be sharing digs again, it's the not having anyone to really...talk to. For some reason you and I...talk in a way that makes me unusually happy,' she finished gruffly, and sipped some wine. 'Even when you were insulting me I enjoyed the challenge.'

'Even when you were insulting me back, so did I,' he murmured.

She grimaced then said slowly, 'It's not that easy to talk to men. Sooner or later—'

'They get a certain look in their eye?' he guessed.

She shrugged.

'Go on.'

'This is a little hard to say.' She pushed her plate away. 'But I couldn't help wondering whether...' She stopped, closed her eyes and wished dearly that she'd never tried to explain.

'The fact that I'm harmless has anything to do with it?'

He said it gravely but there was such a wicked look in his dark eyes, she caught her breath and stared at him with colour rushing into her cheeks.

'I didn't want to, well, hurt your feelings,' she stammered.

He laughed softly. 'My dear Neve, when you've suffered as many physical and mental indignities as

I have, being thought of as harmless is quite mild, believe me.'

She closed her eyes and breathed relievedly. 'Thank heavens!'

'Although I may not be quite as harmless as you imagine,' he added, 'but you're right, I certainly couldn't leap on you and wrestle you to the floor.'

The phone rang before she could think of anything to say. Neve stood up with a frown and went to the table in the hall. It was George Maitland.

'Neve,' he said genially, 'how did it go?'

'...What?' she asked confusedly.

'The party! What else?' he said down the line. 'Now I know it's not your cup of tea, Neve, so I just thought I'd see how you were going. I'd hate to think of you sitting in a sea of crumpled-up bits of paper, gnashing your teeth.'

'George, that doesn't happen these days. Remember computers?'

'Don't be nasty, Neve. Uh, did Rob Stowe get in touch?'

'Oh, yes. Thanks to *you*, I believe.'

George chuckled heartily. 'He's a hard man to say no to! Well, give him my regards. See you on Monday!' He put the phone down.

Neve did grit her teeth, at least, and she came back to the table looking annoyed.

'George checking up on you?' Rob suggested with a grin.

'I'm not sure. George being impossibly nosy is more like it. Where were we?'

Rob laughed at her expression. 'I had just assured you that I couldn't leap on you and wrestle you to the floor.'

Neve rubbed her face. 'I've lost the thread—there are times when George Maitland drives me crazy!'

'Oh, I think he has your best interests at heart,' Rob drawled. 'He told me not to do anything to upset you.'

Neve's violet eyes almost crossed as she tried to imagine her boss going in to bat for her—but why?

'As in how?' she asked bewilderedly.

'Well, he's no fool, George, whatever else he may be,' Rob murmured. 'So he could have divined our interest in each other. Speaking of which, were you trying to tell me that what you feel for me is a meeting of minds?'

'It....' Neve stopped and took a breath. 'Yes.'

He looked at her searchingly for a long moment, so long that she wondered if he could see that part of what she'd said was an evasion. Then he moved restlessly and murmured, 'I wish I could say the same.'

His words hung in the air and she stirred uneasily, then reached for the wine bottle to top up their glasses.

He pushed his plate away and looked at her ironically. 'Do you honestly think I'd have been so—furious last night if that's all it was?'

She recalled his fury when she'd put her hands on his chair at Toni's house and shivered slightly. 'I...don't know what to say.'

'Then I'll say it for you.' He paused and narrowed his eyes. 'Why does one beautiful woman leave you cold whereas another does not? Don't answer.' His lips twisted. 'I'm theorizing. I don't know, but from the moment you walked into my house—as a matter of fact, *before* you walked into my house and virtually told me I could go to hell—'

'What do you mean?' She frowned bewilderedly.

He moved his shoulders. 'I happened to be looking out of my study window and I saw you walking up the pavement. I was moved to instant admiration.'

She gazed at him incredulously.

'Believe me, although much to my surprise, that's exactly how it happened. Until I realized who you must be.'

'You…thought I was…just a passer-by you would never see again?' she said haltingly.

'Yes.' He looked momentarily grim. 'Then when you virtually told me to go to hell—'

'I didn't.' But she still looked dazed.

'Neve, perhaps we're *both* more arrogant than we realize.'

They gazed at each other until she made a reluctant though agreeing gesture with her hands.

'Right. But from that moment on I was struck not only by your manner but your beautiful violet eyes, the smoothness of your skin and the arrangement of your figure in a way that was both mental and very physical.'

Neve sat very still for a moment, looking down, then her lashes lifted and she said shakenly, 'Thank you. I…shouldn't be, but that also makes me very happy, not sure why, well, yes I am.' She paused. 'I think I would very much like to be in love with you—if I let myself think about it but I *can't.*'

He said nothing but slid his hand across the table to cover hers. She stared down at it, lean, long-fingered and surprisingly strong-looking and knew suddenly that you could even fall in love with a man's hands.

Then he sat back and rubbed his temples.

'Are you all right?' she asked concernedly.

'Yep. If I don't go back and tell Jude that you adored her lemon meringue, I'll be in trouble.'

'I'll get it,' she said.

In fact they ate Judy's delicious dessert, discussing that good lady and what a treasure she was. Then Rob made a suggestion.

'I know a coffee bar at The Rocks that specializes in the stuff—you could get addicted to their Vienna coffee.'

Neve frowned. 'It's raining, how would we get to The Rocks, and I make nice coffee, too.'

'I just thought a change of scene might...' He shrugged. 'We could take a taxi, I could cope with that and, it's not pouring. I quite like wet streets and reflected lights.'

Neve looked down at herself.

He grinned wickedly. 'It's not posh. All you'd have to do is throw a coat on. In every other respect...' His gaze flickered from her shining hair to her freshly painted nails. 'You're stunning,' he said simply.

She looked at him with a tinge of colour creeping into her cheeks, but it crossed her mind that explaining about Molly Condren was not going to be easy for him. 'All right,' she said slowly. 'If you really want to.'

'Trust me, Neve.'

It was only raining gently but was cold and crisp with it as they drove to the The Rocks, a historic area across Circular Quay from the Sydney Opera House, below the Harbour Bridge. And the reflected lights on the wet streets gave the city a fairy-tale look.

Rob managed the taxi although he needed his crutches to walk but before long they were seated in a dim, almost cavelike but comfortable café surrounded by a marvellous aroma of coffee, with a candle flickering on the table between them.

Even the short contact with the cold night air had made them both sparkle, Neve thought, as she unwound her scarf and laid her coat over the back of her chair.

There were raindrops in his thick dark hair and on the shoulders of his tweed jacket. But above all he looked intensely alive, and he explained why as he looked around and sniffed appreciatively. 'For so long I couldn't do this kind of thing, it's…it's like being let out of jail.'

She smiled at him with such warmth and understanding, he caught his breath and reached for her hand under the table. They sat like that for a couple of minutes, then he sighed, released her hand and signalled for a waiter to take their order.

It was as if Neve had taken a blow in the region of her heart, to remember what still had to be said…

'Molly,' he said as they were sipping their coffee, 'and I had an affair years ago—don't say it,' he warned as her eyes widened, and he added with a faint grin, 'If you can read my mind, I'm not too bad at reading yours. No, Sydney is not littered with women I've had affairs with. It just so happens that Molly and Toni are good friends despite it.'

Neve raised an eyebrow and stirred the cream through her Vienna coffee. 'You don't seem to be too bad at staying good friends with old flames, if I may say so.'

He looked at her wryly. 'It so happens it was a mutual decision to part. Molly fell in love with another man, she desperately wanted to go overseas to make her name internationally and he happened to be going international, while I needed to stay put.' He paused and thought for a bit. 'Nor was it—how can I put it? It was a relationship we drifted into and I don't honestly think *we* gave much thought to getting married.'

'I see.'

He eyed her.

'I'm not being judgmental,' she said.

'Anyway,' he continued after a moment, 'about three years ago Molly came back with Portia in tow, and her only explanation was that things hadn't worked out with Portia's father. She also came back famous and the old crowd of Bill, Bunny, Toni and so on took her back into their bosom and so did I, as a friend.'

He paused, then said, 'Well, I also helped her to put her affairs in order—Molly is hopeless at that kind of thing, she frequently hasn't got two brass farthings to rub together—so I saw a lot of them. And I don't have to tell you how bewitching Portia can be.'

'No,' Neve agreed.

'Then I had the accident and—' He stopped and looked at a point on the wall above Neve's head. 'I was in hospital for six months and Molly—simply moved in.'

Neve blinked at him.

'I know, but I wasn't in the position to do much about it. I was pretty sure she'd blown her current lot of cash and then of course, I was desperately grateful.'

'Tell me,' Neve said quietly.

He smiled. 'She's unique,' he said, 'despite being so hopeless with money. She used to come to the hospital every day whether I wanted her or not and in the dark days when I didn't think I wanted anyone, she used to go around the place, signing autographs, cheering people up, bringing them flowers and chocolates, ringing their relatives for them...' He stopped and shook his head. 'And of course Portia.'

'She came, too?'

'Oh, yes. She used to bring me jigsaw puzzles, huge puzzles with tiny pieces that drove me round the *bend* until we'd got them finished. She used to read to me and play Scrabble. Then, when I got home, they were there and between them they managed to give my life some meaning. Little things like choosing a good school for Portia, getting her a damned dog because she'd always wanted one.'

'*You* were responsible for Oliver?' Neve asked with a twinkle.

'For my sins, yes,' he said ruefully, 'And things like helping Molly to make the right financial decisions again as well as career decisions—she didn't take any work while I was in hospital.'

He stopped, steepled his fingers under his chin and sighed. 'There was always life and movement in the place, warmth and colour, and suddenly it was a home where I'd never needed one before but did so then. They never ever turned their backs on me even when I was diabolical.'

'I think I know what's coming,' Neve whispered.

He looked at her expressionlessly. 'It's Molly's fervent desire that we get married. I couldn't be so ungrateful as to not grant her that.'

Neve wiped a solitary tear from her cheek and thanked heaven for the dimness. The café was about half full, mostly with couples engrossed in each other. It struck her that she'd gone along with his suggestion to come out for coffee because she'd thought it would make it easier for him to explain about Molly on neutral territory.

The irony was, though, if it had, it certainly hadn't made it easier for her. Because she would have loved for them to have been just as engrossed in each other as the other couples were...

Rob waited until she'd regained her composure then he said with an effort, 'I could never rest easy to think of the mess she might make of her life, and Portia's, who doesn't even appear to know who her father is, without me there. I—' He broke off and grimaced. 'This is a lovely, generous woman who's seen a side of me, and done things for me, few would want to see or do.'

'Look, I understand.' Neve looked around, at the candle between them then, reluctantly, into his eyes again. 'But you're not in love with her?'

'I love Molly, I thought I could even be *in* love with her again until—' He stopped abruptly.

'Would she want that? To be married out of gratitude?' Neve asked slowly.

'I may have some faults but letting her know that wouldn't be one of them, Neve.'

'So you think you could fool her?'

'I've—already done that.'

Their gazes met. 'What have you disagreed about, then?' Neve asked out of a dry throat.

'She doesn't want to wait until I'm walking properly again.'

'Is…is she that easy to fool?'

'Normally not, but it's all been helped along by circumstance. I think she thinks I'm still traumatized and possibly always will be.'

Neve opened her mouth but closed it immediately. How could she ask him if he'd ever thought that Portia was *his* daughter when he obviously had not? He must have good reason not to think it, although surely others had seen the resemblance in their eyes, or had it been a trick of her imagination? But then there was the rapport they shared, he and Portia. There was more than gratitude between them, one would have thought.

'What are you thinking?' he asked.

She smiled meaninglessly. 'That if I wasn't in this equation, I'd say something like, it could be a recipe for disaster.'

'Sometimes marriages of convenience turn out surprisingly well.'

'Until someone else crosses your path,' she said barely audibly.

He smiled without humour. 'Should it look like the faintest possibility, I'll obey my first instincts and get out fast. As we both should have done.' He stopped and sighed.

'I guess so,' she murmured. 'This might be the time to take our own advice.'

They stared at each other.

'But may I give you some advice before—we go?' he said quietly. 'If anyone was in danger of becoming a recluse, I think you were more in danger of it than I was.'

She moved restlessly. 'I've only been in town for a few months.'

'Even so, live a little. I'm not saying rush out and jump into bed with the first man who comes your way, but don't let your puritan background put you off completely.'

'You...would be happy to see me with someone else?' she said, and there was an incredulous glint in her violet eyes.

'No. But I'd be happy to see you happy. Because I think you might have been more right than you knew when you said it was *mostly* a meeting of minds from your point of view—for one thing, I'm sure it's hard to get too excited about an old crock like me.' He smiled crookedly. 'It's OK, you don't have to reassure me to the contrary.'

Neve couldn't find any words to say, but it seemed he didn't expect any because he added, 'And of course, from a purely selfish point of view, then I would really know I couldn't have you.'

CHAPTER FOUR

A MONTH later Neve stopped what she was doing suddenly, which was writing a weekly column on the latest movies to be released—another of Brent Madison's tasks she'd had to take over—to find George Maitland breathing down her neck and staring at the screen of the computer she was working on.

'You wanted something, George?'

'No, no! Well, just to congratulate you since you took over the movie column, Neve. You certainly have an original eye for it.'

'I've seen more movies in the last few weeks than in whole lifetime,' she said with a grin.

'And you're about to see one more, kid, but get out your glad rags this time. This is no preview but a full-blown premiere in aid of charity on Saturday night, and you're invited to it.'

'As a working journalist I have no doubt,' Neve murmured.

'You can still dress up! I'm planning a full page for it with your review of the movie as well as pics of the cream of Sydney society who will no doubt be attending, and their comments afterwards. It's that big-budget adventure movie there's been so much hoo-haa about.'

'OK—'

'And I do mean dress up, Neve. I want you in

something long and glamorous because I'm planning to include you in the pics.'

'I haven't got—all right, George,' Neve said laughingly as her editor donned his most mulish look.

'How's the Stone interview coming along?' he asked. Jason Stone had recently won the Booker Prize for literature.

'Well, no problem getting him to talk,' Neve replied wryly. 'The opposite, if anything. Sorting the dross from the gold is another matter.'

'I always thought he was too full of himself for words. I imagine he'll be impossible now. So, when can I expect the finished article?'

Neve sighed. 'As soon as I can do it, George. Is there any word of Brent coming back?'

'Glandular fever can take months.'

'It's already been over a month.'

'He's convalescing in the Seychelles.'

Neve's mouth dropped open.

George laughed. 'He had some leave accumulated. He's also bringing back all the gen on the place.'

'Half his luck,' Neve said bitterly. 'When do I get to do travel?'

'I might think about it when Brent does come back. Yes, I will. In the meantime, keep up the good work, Neve.' He hesitated, looked at her with a strange intensity as if he was dying to ask her something but he, in the end, only patted her on her shoulder. He had no idea how dark her gaze was as it rested on his departing back.

But it wasn't until that night that Neve got the opportunity to reflect that even if she'd wanted to confide in someone, it wouldn't be George. And to reflect that, even if she'd wanted to take Rob Stowe's advice, given just before they'd parted to take separate taxis home from The Rocks without saying much more at all, she'd scarcely had a free minute to do so.

She got home late from work, dropped her bag onto her bed and went to take a shower. Spring was coming to Sydney in a burst of unusually warm, sticky weather. She'd been warned not to take this generous burst of warmth too seriously, there was sure to be more cold weather around the corner, they said, but wrapped in a cool seersucker robe after her shower, she leant out of her bedroom window and enjoyed the balmy night.

Until, that was, something drew her gaze to the vague direction of Woollahra, and as they had the habit of doing when she was least expecting it, thoughts of Rob Stowe flooded her mind.

She retreated from the window, poured herself a glass of pineapple juice, and relaxed in an armchair with the familiar dilemma she still had not solved.

Had he really meant what he'd said about her being more right than she knew? That for her it was only a meeting of minds? Or had he said it to make it easier for her?

She'd never know, she reflected. Although, despite anything he'd said, despite describing himself as an 'old crock'—something she'd never thought of him—she was pretty sure she'd fallen in love with him.

There wouldn't be this lonely, aching place within her, she reasoned, otherwise. There wouldn't be a genuine aversion to doing what he'd suggested whereas before it had not been something she'd bothered much about one way or the other.

She wouldn't be feeling astonishment, she mused with a slight grimace, when she remembered the couple of times she'd thought she was in love before. Because those men had never entered her heart and soul as he had.

She drained her glass and set it down beside her. And forced herself to think along different lines— ones that would heal her eventually, she hoped. Even at the time she was meeting Rob, it had had a dream-like quality to it. To fall in love with a man in the space of only four meetings didn't seem rational, did it? And how much had his unattainability contributed to it? How enchanted, now, was distance making the view look?

'Absence making the heart grow fonder, all those platitudes,' she murmured with distaste, 'but could they be true? I sincerely hope so.'

She laid her head back and wondered whether they were married yet. Had Molly got her way? She had no doubt it wouldn't have been a broadcast event. Would that make it easier for her, she wondered and echoed his words—*Then I'd know I couldn't have you.*

But no answer came to her, and with a sigh she forced herself to go over her notes on the Stone interview.

On Saturday morning she rushed out to buy a long dress.

On Saturday evening as they waited outside the theatre, the cameraman she was with said admiringly,

'Neve, you should do this more often. You look stunning.'

'Thank you, Will. You don't look too bad yourself!' They'd worked together a lot, she and Will Gibson, and she'd always found him easy, pleasant and more than happy to discuss his four children with her. 'Thank heavens it's not cold,' she added as she squinted down at herself.

The dress was silk organza over a taffeta underslip. The organza was a creamy colour with big, shadowy violet blue flowers and the style was slim about her figure with one shoulder bare and a froth of organza where it was caught up on the other shoulder.

Her hair was drawn back at the sides and fastened at the back with a violet blue bow. Her shoes were cream kid with very high heels. If it hadn't been for the tape recorder in her hands, she could have been a bona fide guest at this premiere in aid of charity.

'Here we go!' Will said. 'First limo arriving.'

'I hope you know who they all are,' Neve remarked, 'because I certainly don't.'

'It's always the same old crowd,' he responded somewhat cynically.

'All right, I'm just going to chat my impressions onto the tape, if you could tell me who they are. It's when they come out I'll need to collar some of them.'

For half an hour a stream of limos deposited the rich and famous on the red-carpeted pavement. Then there was a lull and Will said, 'Looks like that's it! Hang on.' And he whistled softly. 'Now there's a scoop, Neve! Rob Stowe in company with, of all people, Molly Condren and a kid. Neve?' He looked around. 'You hiding or something?'

'Yes,' she said desperately, uncaring of what he must think. 'Just stand in front of me. I don't want them to see me.'

He looked at her for an instant as if she'd gone round the bend then moved so that he was blocking her more effectively. Fortunately he was a tall, well-built man.

But although she may not have been visible, and Rob, Molly and Portia passed into the theatre obviously unaware that she was there, she had been able to peep out from behind Will and see them.

Rob in a dark dinner suit and white shirt, walking with only the aid of a stick. Molly, with a complicated upswept hairstyle, absolutely glowing in rich chartreuse silk. And Portia wore a pearly white, high-necked, long-sleeved dress with a green sash, white tights, white patent-leather shoes and green ribbons in her loose hair.

'Want to tell me about it?'

Neve started.

'Thought you knew him? Didn't you do the interview? I did the pics. He was really easy to work with.'

'Unfortunately, Will,' Neve said, 'we…clashed a bit.'

'Must have been a lot to provoke that reaction in you, Neve,' Will said. 'OK. Shall we go and watch this movie? It's not often I get a free ticket.'

Three hours later Neve said to Will as the credits closed, 'I don't know about you but I'm exhausted—talk about action!'

The lights came on and the audience rose applauding loudly.

'I thought it was great,' Will said enthusiastically. 'Oh, well, back to work. I'll get my camera and meet you in the foyer.'

'Just do me a favour, Will. Stay away from Rob Stowe if you see him, them.'

He looked at her quizzically but nodded.

'...May I quote you?' Neve asked for about the tenth time, this time of a raddled, elderly woman dripping in the finest diamonds she'd ever seen.

'Yes, yes!' the woman answered. 'Damn fine movie, but then I've always had a yen for—' She named the male lead in the film.

'Is that so—I beg your pardon.' She turned as someone said her name, to find Portia standing behind her smiling widely.

'Neve! I'm so glad to see you! You do look stunning. How's your ankle? Did you enjoy the movie? I thought it was simply smashing!'

'Darling—there you are! You shouldn't go off on your own—why, Neve!' Molly Condren said delightedly as she loomed up behind Portia. 'How wonderful to see you again. You know, I always wanted to tell you that I thought the interview you did with Rob was excellent. You got it so right and you got him so right—didn't she, darling?' she added mischievously as Rob appeared at her side.

Neve made a gesture to Will, a negative gesture, and he lowered his camera immediately. 'Thank you, Molly,' she said. 'It's nice to see you again. And you, Portia—'

'Are you working?' Portia asked excitedly.

'Uh—yes, I'm supposed to be asking people what

they thought of the movie. The magazine is going to do an article on it—'

'Oh, do ask me! I can, can't I, Rob?'

For the first time Neve looked directly at Rob. 'I'm sorry,' she said helplessly. 'I—'

'How are you, Neve?' he broke in easily. 'You don't look as if you're working.'

'This is George's idea—I'm supposed to feature in the article myself.'

'Well, you look good enough to come on to the party we're giving, Neve,' Molly put in. 'Why don't you, we'd love to have you, wouldn't we, Rob?'

This was like a nightmare, Neve thought. 'Thank you so much but I'm...I'm actually going out to dinner myself. *We* are, aren't we, Will?'

'Er...' Will flinched slightly as Neve stood on his toe. 'Yes. Yes!'

Molly looked genuinely disappointed and so did Portia. 'But could you still interview me, Neve?' Portia said. 'As a kid I could have a different perspective.'

'I don't see why not,' Molly said gaily, but Neve was watching Rob.

'Then I'll leave you two to it,' he only murmured wryly and moved away.

So Neve got both Molly's and Portia's comments on the movie, and they both were photographed. Then they chatted for a few minutes until Molly said she better go and rescue Rob, and they said goodbye.

'Don't,' Neve said to Will. 'I mean, don't ask for any explanations, it's just one of those things. I'm sorry.' She smiled ruefully at him.

'It's OK, but much as I'd like to take you to dinner,

Neve, I am a married man and it does so happen to be my wife's birthday today. It's getting late, so—'

'Will, I made all that up on the spur of the moment,' she confessed. 'You go. I'll grab a cab.'

'Sure? I can drop you off somewhere—'

'No, I think we live in opposite directions, but thanks all the same, Will,' she said sincerely.

Still he hesitated. 'You don't want to go trooping around on your own looking like that, Neve.'

'I left my coat and bag with the manager, I really will be fine, Will!'

It took her five minutes to locate the manager and retrieve her things by which time the red carpet was rolled up and all the glamorous guests had left. Neve stood on the pavement as they locked the doors behind her, with her mobile phone in her hand, only to sigh in sheer frustration as she suddenly became aware why it wasn't responding—the battery was dead and she'd forgotten to bring a spare.

Then, to her amazement, a limo that had been driving past, stopped abruptly and reversed into the kerb opposite her, and Molly looked out of the window.

'Neve, are you all right? What happened to your escort?'

'He…he got called away, a…an emergency,' Neve stammered, 'but—'

Portia popped her head out. 'Then you can come to the party—yippee!'

'Yes, do get in, Neve, we've got plenty of room,' Molly enthused.

Toni was at the party in a slinky black gown with her fair hair like a polished helmet. Bill and Bunny

Fanshawe were there, Bunny having adopted a lay-
ered look with none of the improbable garments
she'd donned matching, and there were about twenty
other people who'd been to the premiere.

Judy served a delicious finger supper and champagne flowed.

'It's not possible to ignore each other all evening,'
Rob Stowe said quietly to her at one stage.

She looked up into his dark eyes. 'No. I'm sorry
about this, though.'

'I think you were simply outgunned by fate tonight.'

'Perhaps,' she murmured, and took a sip of champagne. 'It's good to see you so mobile,' she added.
He was on his feet although propped against the back
of a chair with his stick in reach.

'I've made some giant strides in the last month or
so. Funnily enough, they told me I was getting towards the end of a long haul but I didn't quite believe
them.' He grimaced.

'Does that mean you'll soon be able to do all the
things you used to do?'

'Not quite,' he said wryly. 'But at least I'm not
confined to that damned chair or crutches anymore.'

'Have you taken the other giant step?'

Their gazes locked and he didn't pretend to mis-
understand. 'Not yet, but the date has been set.'

'She looks so lovely and so happy, they both do,'
Neve said.

He made no comment on that. He said instead,
'Did you really have a date with the photographer?'

Neve felt the warmth that tinged her cheeks faintly
pink and knew it was useless to lie. 'He's a married

man with four children and it's his wife's birthday—
no, I made it up on the spur of the moment.'

He looked briefly amused. 'Is there anyone?'

'Rob, what difference does it make?' She looked
at him steadily.

He gave her one swift but nevertheless, compre-
hensive glance that took in the velvety skin of her
bare shoulder, the slimness of her figure beneath the
lovely dress then the look in her violet eyes before
he said, 'You're right, none. Well, shall we circu-
late?'

'By all means,' she agreed.

After that the evening seemed interminable although there was one bright spot when Molly drew
her aside and asked her if she'd mind having a look
at Portia's essay book. Portia was standing beside her
first on one foot then the other.

'Uh—of course. Are you interested in writing,
Portia?'

'Immensely,' Portia responded. 'It's my ambition
to be just like you.'

As they left the room, Neve was conscious of
Rob's eyes on her back, so she was feeling not only
uneasy but surprised as well at Portia's statement
when they reached her room. Then there was the
room itself, which was luxurious to say the least.

Portia had a single bed with a white coverlet and
a draped hanging suspended from the wall behind it
in folds of a silvery gossamer fabric. The carpet was
cyclamen pink, the walls jade green, and in one corner there sat a wonderful, soft harlequin doll that was
as big as she was.

There was also a lovely teak desk and chair.

'I like your room,' Neve said.

'Thanks—Mum did it. I thought she'd gone a bit over the top for a twelve-year-old, to be honest, but I've got used to it now. Rob gave me the doll, isn't he gorgeous?' She picked up the harlequin and hugged him then sat him back and led Neve by the hand to the desk. 'This is my last one. I got an A+ for it.'

Neve read the two-page essay in Portia's big, round hand with growing respect.

'What do you think?'

'I think you've got a way with words, Portia.' Neve paged through the book reading excerpts from other essays. 'Does your school have a magazine?'

'Yes, but it's only the older girls who contribute.'

'If you want to be a writer,' Neve said slowly, 'there are two things you have to do. Assess the market and keep sending things in, so give it a try. Also, most papers have children's pages, I know we do in the Sunday edition. They publish letters, poems and stories. Why don't you try that?'

Portia jumped up and down excitedly then she sobered. 'The only thing is, when you've got an essay to write, it's easy. You've got a subject. Otherwise, I don't seem to know where to start.'

'How about starting with Oliver? You could almost write a book about him. Or the movie you saw today and what impression it made on you. Then there's your lovely harlequin doll, the kind of food you like—or hate. The clothes you like to wear, the clothes you think grown-ups look silly in, perhaps.'

Neve stopped as Portia stared at her wide-eyed with growing excitement, and said, 'Why didn't I think of that?'

'You can't be expected to think of everything when you're only twelve!'

Portia sighed. 'I do like you so much, Neve.'

When the party at last began to break up, Molly looked around and asked Toni if she'd mind giving Neve a lift home.

'Oh, I can get a taxi,' Neve protested, but neither Molly nor Tony would hear of it. And Rob said goodbye to her quite casually although still with that hint of something narrow and assessing in his eyes as had greeted her when she'd come back downstairs with Portia.

'They've set the date,' Toni said as she drove her yellow Porsche through the streets of Sydney.

'I know.'

Toni raised an eyebrow at her. 'I didn't think it was public knowledge.'

'Rob told me this evening,' Neve said quietly. 'Not the date, just—that it was happening.'

'So nothing came about between you two?'

'No.'

'Pity—I don't think he's doing the right thing.'

Neve looked out of the window and tried to sound impersonal as she said, 'He may feel that it's the best thing for all of them.'

'Strange how blind men can be,' Toni murmured as she pulled up outside Neve's block of flats.

'You mean...do you mean...?' Neve broke off and bit her lip.

'I mean Portia,' Toni said flatly. 'You only have to look at them, don't tell me it didn't strike you?'

'Yes,' Neve confessed, 'as soon as I saw them

together, well, it didn't *strike* me but it made me wonder. But if she is his child, why hasn't Molly told him? Why doesn't he suspect?'

'Molly—don't get me wrong, I love her—but she is a highly disorganized person. Perhaps it's that star quality, but she's not only hopeless with her finances but also her emotions and, until recently, her love life. So while Rob *could* have been the father, she was quite sure it was the man she went overseas with all those years ago, with whom she thought she was madly in love, but who then dropped her like a ton of bricks when he found out about the baby.'

'I…how did she cope?' Neve asked.

'Her parents. They flew over and helped pick up the pieces. Then they looked after Portia while Molly got her career going again.'

'So, does Molly still not know whose child Portia is—she must by now!'

'She said it came like the kick of a mule one day, up until then Portia had so much resembled her—but that might have been due to the red hair. She said…' Toni paused and looked heavenwards. 'She could only ever tell Rob if he married her of his own free will.'

Neve stared at her speechlessly.

'You have to make allowances for Molly, Neve. She just doesn't seem to work on the same wavelengths that more rational people do. But she's so loving and generous and lovely…' Toni stopped and shrugged.

'Well, she obviously thinks he's marrying her of his own free will—I mean—'

'And not out of gratitude and because he can't tear himself away from Portia anyway? Precisely.

Strange, isn't it? Especially when the rest of us can see it so clearly.'

Neve took a breath. 'You could all be quite wrong. In expecting it to fail, I mean. Because it's not only Portia he can't tear himself away from. He can't bear to think of Molly muddling through as she's obviously so renowned for.'

'Is that why you've retired from the lists?'

Neve swallowed. 'Yes. And if fate should at last choose to be kind to me, I won't have to go through this kind of thing again.'

Toni patted her hand. 'I believe dear Brent is due to be returned to our midst?'

Neve grimaced. 'You know more than I do! I thought he was in the Seychelles.'

'He was. He came back yesterday, panting to get into the swing of things.'

'Thank heavens—I might be relieved of the social pages at least.'

'Are you working on anything else?' Toni asked curiously.

'Several things but the one that's giving me headaches is an article on rare stamps.'

'My dear Neve—did you know my father collected them? I have, to put it mildly, a rare old collection of rare stamps. Why don't you come and have lunch with me—let's see, how about Monday?'

On Sunday afternoon, her doorbell rang and once again it was Rob but this time under his own steam and standing.

'What—why?' she stammered.

'Just let me in, Neve,' he said impatiently.

She hesitated then fumbled with the chain.

'Not still housekeeping?' he queried dryly as he followed her into the lounge.

'If you've come here to insult me, Rob Stowe—'

'On the contrary,' he said curtly, 'I've come to tell you that I've been a blind, absolute bloody fool, but did you have to?'

Neve blinked. 'I don't know what you're talking about.'

He looked her up and down. The warm weather had persisted and she wore a calf-length floral cotton skirt, a pink knit shirt with a scoop neckline and short sleeves, sandals and her hair was tied back in a ponytail. He himself was casually dressed in khaki cotton trousers and a plain blue shirt, but she thought he looked pale.

'Don't you? Who else would have speculated on it even if you didn't put it into the interview? None of my friends I can assure you, although why none of them tried to tell me—' He broke off and swore violently. 'Then there was the way you disappeared with her last night.'

Neve's lips parted as a glimmer of understanding came to her. 'You don't mean...you mean Portia?'

'Of course I mean Portia,' he said scathingly. 'I'm told it struck you as soon as you saw us together. And now,' he added menacingly, 'it's common knowledge.'

Neve put her hand on the back of a chair for the simple reason that for the first time in her life she felt like fainting. 'You think I did that?' she said barely audibly.

'Why else would I get a call from a journalist from your bloody paper this morning, asking me if I'd like to comment on the rumour that Portia was my daughter?'

'It's not my...' She swallowed and started again. 'The only person I have *ever* spoken to about this is Toni. And she brought it up last night when she drove me home.'

'So it didn't strike you as soon as you saw us together?' He was still pale, with suppressed fury, she realized.

'Yes,' she cried. 'But it was Toni, not me, who commented on how *blind* men can be. Is that why you're so angry, Rob? And looking for a scapegoat?'

For a moment she thought he was going to strike her. Then he leant his stick against the chair, shot out a hand and pulled her into his arms. 'I've wanted to do this since I first saw you, Neve, but don't take it as a compliment, will you?' he murmured, and started to kiss her.

She didn't respond but she didn't fight, either, because one small part of her mind, she was amazed to discover, was more concerned with the damage he could do if he lost his balance.

But when he raised his head abruptly, she said, 'If you've quite finished, I think you should go.'

He kept her in his arms, however, with surprising strength, although he swivelled round so that he had the wall to lean against. He also said with supreme irony, 'Is that why you're still a virgin, Neve? Because you're basically cold?'

She kept her temper with difficulty. 'No. Did you seriously expect me to respond to brute force and insults? Nor should you take too much for granted, Mr. Stowe. It's only because of your fragile back that

I haven't adopted a course of action my brothers recommended in these circumstances.'

He laughed. 'Ah—some complicated karate move?' he hazarded.

'Much cruder than that.'

'Makes the eyes water to think of it,' he said gravely.

'You haven't let me go,' Neve pointed out.

'My back is still as fragile as it was two minutes ago. And I'm not too easy to restore to my feet once I fall flat, I should warn you.'

'Stop it!' Neve ordered, now as pale as he had been. 'You come here and accuse me of terrible things, think you can kiss me in a way that is only demeaning and—'

'Kissing you, even in a rage, Neve, is quite an experience. As is holding you—so you deny the charge?' His dark eyes were no longer violently angry or scathing, but quite serious and probing.

Neve, however, got even angrier. 'Damn it,' she said through her teeth. 'Who do you think you are! I don't propose to have any kind of a conversation with you in this situation, and I don't propose to grovel to you with explanations of why it wasn't me. If you could believe it in the first place, you can go to hell, Rob Stowe.'

'You're trembling,' he said quietly, and moved his hands on her back, although still giving her no chance to escape.

'Not from anything other than a desire to flatten you if I could!'

'What if I said I was sorry?'

'You can still go to hell.' She stared at him proudly.

He considered for a moment then he said barely audibly, 'I'm in hell anyway.' And started to kiss her again.

FREE GIFTS!

NO COST! NO OBLIGATION TO BUY!
NO PURCHASE NECESSARY!

DETACH AND MAIL CARD TODAY!

PLAY THE
Lucky Key Game

Scratch gold area with a coin.
Then check below to see the gifts you get!

YES! I have scratched off the gold area. Please send me the 2 Free
books and gift for which I qualify. I understand I am under no obligation to
purchase any books, as explained on the back and on the opposite page.

306 HDL CX9X   **106 HDL CX9M**

Name
_____
(PLEASE PRINT CLEARLY)

Address _____ Apt.# _____

City _____ State/Prov. _____ Postal Zip/Code _____

| 🔑🔑🔑🔑 | 2 free books plus a mystery gift | 🔑🔑🔑🔑 | 1 free book |
| 🔑🔑🔑🔑 | 2 free books | 🔑🔑🔑🔑 | Try Again! |

Offer limited to one per household and not valid to
current Harlequin Presents® subscribers.
All orders subject to approval.

(H-P-01/00)
PRINTED IN U.S.A.

The Harlequin Reader Service® — Here's how it works:

Accepting your 2 free books and gift places you under no obligation to buy anything. You may keep the books and gift and return the shipping statement marked "cancel." If you do not cancel, about a month later we'll send you 6 additional novels and bill you just $3.12 each in the U.S., or $3.49 each in Canada, plus 25¢ delivery per book and applicable taxes if any.* That's the complete price and — compared to cover prices of $3.75 each in the U.S. and $4.25 each in Canada — it's quite a bargain! You may cancel at any time, but if you choose to continue, every month we'll send you 6 more books, which you may either purchase at the discount price or return to us and cancel your subscription.

*Terms and prices subject to change without notice. Sales tax applicable in N.Y. Canadian residents will be charged applicable provincial taxes and GST.

If offer card is missing write to: Harlequin Reader Service, 3010 Walden Ave., P.O. Box 1867, Buffalo NY 14240-1867

BUSINESS REPLY MAIL
FIRST-CLASS MAIL   PERMIT NO. 717   BUFFALO, NY

POSTAGE WILL BE PAID BY ADDRESSEE

HARLEQUIN READER SERVICE
3010 WALDEN AVE
PO BOX 1867
BUFFALO NY 14240-9952

NO POSTAGE
NECESSARY
IF MAILED
IN THE
UNITED STATES

CHAPTER FIVE

'No...'

It was a whispered protest but this was no angry, humiliating kiss, this was something else all together she soon found. He nuzzled the soft curve of her neck where it joined her shoulder, then he crossed his hands over her back, spreading his fingers and drawing her into the tall, lean length of him.

And she suddenly went boneless in his arms as her senses were assaulted by the touch, the feel and the taste of him. There was an instant of respite as they looked into each other's eyes but the sensation of sheer intimacy she had with this man was heightened because she could see utter absorption with her in their dark, heavy-lidded depths.

And she could feel her body responding to his as his hands were gentle on it, feel her breasts starting to ache with desire, and feel her hands as if they had a life of their own, longing to trace the line of his shoulders beneath the blue cotton, to smooth the skirt away as a flush of heat ran through her. And a lovely languorous excitement made her move against him and make a small, husky sound in her throat.

He kissed her deeply and she responded until she felt almost dizzy with rapture, as well as dizzy with the knowledge that there could be only one satisfactory end to this delight, and that would be to go to bed with him.

They drew apart at last and with a sigh, his hands dropped to his side. Neve laid her head on his chest for one bittersweet moment and he slid his fingers through hers and raised them to his lips. Then they parted completely, she to walk over to the window with her arms wrapped about her as if for comfort, he to limp over to a chair.

'I'm sorry,' he said finally. 'For everything, for suspecting you of—I've been in such a state of shock since it happened.'

Neve turned. 'I can imagine. Was it only—shock?'

'It was—no, it wasn't only shock. It was like one of Portia's own jigsaw puzzles. As if I'd been searching for the missing piece without even realizing it. How could I have been such a fool?' He laid his head back wearily.

'My mother used to say she had six children and none of them looked like her, but of course most of us do to varying degrees, she just can't see it.'

He looked at her sombrely. 'Why the hell didn't she tell me—don't answer. Toni—I rang Toni immediately, because I thought she'd at least be honest with me however belatedly—and she was.'

'So that's how you thought it was me?'

'She said, in the course of the conversation that it had even made a complete stranger like you stop and think.'

'I didn't say a word to anyone apart from Toni,' Neve said intensely.

'I believe you. It just seemed such a coincidence coming from—how the hell do you think it did...come about?'

'Have you ever been out and about with Portia and Molly before?' Neve asked slowly.

'Yes, of course, but not—do you mean occasions such as the premiere? No,' he answered, 'and that wasn't my idea, but Molly was dying to go. So I thought, well, everyone's accused me of becoming a recluse.' He grimaced. 'Do you think someone noticed it and contacted the paper or...?'

Neve spread her hands. 'If you tell me who rang, I can find out for you.'

He shrugged. 'It's not going to make much difference now.'

'It would clear my name.'

'I told you, I believe you.'

There was a long silence then Neve sat down opposite him. 'How have they taken it?'

'Molly and Portia? They don't know. They've gone to the school fête.'

'You must—I know how fond you are of her— you must be delighted too,' she said sincerely.

He raised those dark eyes to her. 'I *am*,' he said intensely. 'I had this pang of pure joy before all the rest of it hit me. I...always did love her as if she were my own kid. I'd do anything for Portia.' He paused. 'But I'm also more trapped now than ever.' He smiled but with no humour. 'Do you know why I fell so easily into the trap of believing *you* had spilt the beans?'

Neve stared at him with a frown in her eyes.

'So I could say to myself—OK, that's it! If she could do this then there can never be anything of value between us and I'm a fool to imagine I still want her.'

Neve's lips twisted and she stood up again. 'Have you made love to a woman since the accident, Rob?'

'No.'

'Can...' She stopped and bit her lip.

'Can I?' He lay back in the chair again and watched her with that narrow glance she knew well. 'Yes I can. In a restrained sort of way.'

'Then, not even with...?' Again she stopped awkwardly.

'No, Neve, not even with Molly.' His eyes were suddenly sardonic. 'What's your point?'

'I think you may be a dangerously frustrated man, Rob.'

He sat up abruptly and swore.

'Perhaps even worried about how it will go after so long,' she said steadily.

He gazed at her incredulously.

She swallowed but made herself go on. 'I do know a bit about it, I didn't only research *you* for the interview but all sorts of problems associated with paraplegia even when it's temporary, and that's a special area that can be very tricky.'

'Are you saying—' he eyed her dangerously '—I'm not sure I'm quite up to it and I'm using you to...' He stopped dead and stood up to tower over her.

She winced inwardly but went on. 'I'm saying that you and Molly go way back and have everything to go *forward* for. Just let her...deal with it. I'm sure she can, with love and laughter. And then you'll wonder what you ever saw in me.'

'Neve,' he said through his teeth, 'that wasn't what you were saying ten minutes ago.'

She shrugged delicately. 'When you're accused of being frigid, you tend to want to prove you aren't.'

'Are you serious?'

'Deadly serious,' she responded. 'You see, you

were right about me. I would love to spend my life talking to you, but living with you—no. And I think I'm right about you. You not only need Molly, you love her but you're—wary about taking the final step. And don't forget...' She smiled quietly although her heart felt as if it was breaking. 'There's a lot of Molly in Portia, too. Go home, Rob, and marry her, and don't take no for an answer.'

'You seem to be very sure of what you're doing,' he said grimly.

She turned away briefly but when she turned back, her violet eyes were dry and steady. 'I am.'

He walked out without a word.

'You know, I thought there'd have been some mention of it in the gossip columns,' Toni said over lunch the next day.

'George killed it,' Neve said as she ate ginger chicken on a bed of rice in Toni's veranda room with the harbour spread out seemingly at their feet.

The warm weather had abated as predicted and a cool westerly was whipping up the waters of the harbour.

'George Maitland—how did he know?' Toni asked.

'I told him. He's a friend of Rob's, as you probably know.'

Toni sipped her wine and said, 'I couldn't believe it when Rob rang me in this absolute state and asked whether I knew if it was true. Then he proceeded to verbally pulverise me for not telling him. Men! Heaven alone knows what will happen now.'

'Oh, I think it will all go ahead as planned.'

Toni glanced at her intently. But she said, 'You

don't know Molly. Not that well, I mean. And even
if George has canned it, people are out there talking
about it. It has to become common knowledge so if
Rob tries to pretend he doesn't know...' She
shrugged.

'I'm sure he wouldn't do that.'

'I always told Molly she should have come clean
as soon as she realized, you know.'

'Toni.' Neve pushed away her plate. 'Thank you
for a delicious lunch. Tell me how your father got
into stamp collecting?'

'I see,' Toni murmured. 'End of subject—sorry,
it's obviously a bit painful for you.'

Neve said nothing.

'My father—' Toni touched a napkin to her mouth
'—when he made a lot of money looked around for
a hobby that would be "gentlemanly." He was actually addicted to all sorts of less than upper class
pursuits, gambling on the dogs, pub darts, beer drink-
ing and rugby league. My mother suggested stamps,
but it was only when he realized how valuable rare
stamps were that he became seriously interested.
Once that happened, it grew to be a mania with him.
Let me show you.'

Neve got home much later that afternoon silently
blessing Antonia Simpson because she now had more
than enough material for her article, plus, Toni had
allowed her to photograph some of her father's
stamps.

She'd also agreed to Neve using him as background for the article and had told her about one of
his great rivals, now dead, too. They'd conducted
legendary bidding battles when rare stamps had come

up for auction and it had brought each of them personal pain to think of the other owning a rarer stamp.

She made herself a light meal then took a cup of coffee to her desk and turned her computer on. Three hours later, she rubbed her neck and her eyes but was satisfied with what she'd hammered out. And she went to bed and fell asleep immediately.

The next morning George scanned her copy leisurely then he sat up and said, not in a leisurely way at all, 'You didn't!'

Neve raised an eyebrow at him.

'How the hell did you get access to the Simpson collection?' he asked excitedly.

'Well, I didn't break in, if that's what you thought,' she said with an imp of humour dancing in her eyes.

'Neve, don't joke about it. I've been trying to—for years I've been trying to—is this legit? I mean, she did give her permission?'

'Of course she did, George.'

'Why?'

It was a question Neve had asked herself and the answer she'd come up with had been slightly discomforting—did Toni feel guilty about bringing her and Rob together again? 'Uh, I think she's just taken a liking to me, George. By the way,' she added swiftly, 'I believe Brent is back?'

'Yes, starts work next Monday,' George said distractedly then he looked up at her. 'Why?'

'Just wondered.'

He gazed at her thoughtfully. 'How's the Stone interview going?'

'I'll have it on your desk tomorrow morning.'

'Beauty! By the way, I rang Rob Stowe and apologized. Told him how it had happened, an anonymous call to the social pages, not of the mag, but the main paper. Of course, the crazy part about it is, all of us who know him have been wondering for the last three years!'

'So—I believe.'

'How did you get to know about it, Neve?' George asked with an intent little frown. 'I mean—to be able to tip me off the way you did?'

'He—' Neve thought quickly '—he wondered whether I had…anything to do with it. You know, noticed it when I met Portia the day the dog knocked me over.'

'Did you?'

'George, yes, it did make me stop and think, but no, I had nothing to do with it.'

'I'm not accusing you of it, Neve.' George looked hurt.

She shrugged.

'I see,' George said, apropos of absolutely nothing. Neve lost her patience. *'What?'*

'That you need a break, my dear Neve, and I propose to give you one! Take next week off. To be perfectly honest, Brent looks the picture of health, so much so, one is forced to wonder whether he wasn't, well, making the best of his glandular fever. No.' He held up his hand as Neve started to protest. 'I insist. Why don't you take yourself to the Seychelles? Marvellously efficacious kind of place I would say.'

When she got home that night, Neve went straight to her dressing table mirror and stared at herself critically. Did she look ill or particularly stressed out, she wondered. Haggard? Not that she could see anything amiss, although, on further consideration, there were faint blue shadows beneath her eyes and she hadn't needed George to tell her that she'd lost a bit of weight.

She sat down on the end of the bed and wrapped her arms around herself. And now George, who could be an absolute slave driver at times, had taken away her one prop—work. The one thing she'd relied on to get her through this awful time of knowing that she'd deliberately lied to Rob Stowe. That she'd done the one thing most calculated to drive him into Molly Condren's arms.

She'd had no choice, she reminded herself. She could never have lived with the thought of separating him from Portia. And she wasn't a hundred per cent sure that she hadn't hit the nail on the head about Rob himself anyway, she mused.

It occurred to her suddenly to wonder more about Molly Condren. The real substance of this woman everyone loved—when they weren't tearing their hair out over her. The woman who had walked out on Rob Stowe for another man, virtually going from one bed to the other so she couldn't be sure who was the father of her child.

But she obviously hadn't been planning a child, something must have gone wrong with her contraception or was she *that* disorganized?

But why was she even thinking this, Neve asked herself, and jumped as someone knocked on the front door.

It couldn't be, she told herself. Not Rob again.

It wasn't—it was his daughter.

'Portia! What are you doing here? Does...do...?'

Neve's eyes widened further as they fell on a bag at Portia's feet. The girl was dressed in her tartan leggings and green jumper but she also had a coat over her arm.

'Please let me in, Neve,' Portia begged. 'There's no one else I can go to, not anyone sensible, at least.'

'But...all right.' Neve opened the door and Portia picked up her bag and came in. 'But I have to let your...I have to let your mother and Rob know you're here, you do understand that, don't you, Portia? They'll be out of their minds.'

'No they won't, not yet at least. I'm supposed to be at my drama class until eight-thirty.'

'But your drama teacher—'

'Oh, she'll be reading Shakespeare, once she gets into that she loses all sense of reality. I like your flat.' Portia looked around. 'When I'm a journalist I'll have one just like it.'

Neve closed the front door dazedly. 'How did you know where I lived?'

'I looked in Rob's directory. I was going to ring your paper,' she confided, 'because I couldn't find you in the phone book, but I didn't have to. The thing is, Neve, I need to talk to someone. My whole world has changed dramatically—you're not going to believe this but after all these years I now have a father.'

Neve stared into her glowing dark eyes and felt the sting of tears in her own. She blinked them away and said, 'Portia, congratulations!' She held out her hand and Portia shook it gravely.

'The funny thing is,' Portia continued, 'I sometimes dreaded meeting my father because I knew I could never love him as I love Rob and now...isn't it amazing?'

'I'm very happy for you. As fathers go, I doubt if you could have a better one.'

Portia glowed again. Then she sobered. 'There's a down side to it, though. Grown-ups are really strange sometimes. They're arguing about who did the right thing and who didn't, whether they should get married or not, and all sorts of things.'

'In front of you?' Neve asked incredulously.

'No, of course not but...' Portia looked slightly wary, 'I'm very good at listening at doors.'

'I see.' Neve's lips trembled. 'You shouldn't, though.'

'How else does a twelve-year-old get into the picture?' Portia asked aggrievedly.

'There are some pictures you might be too young to be in,' Neve suggested carefully.

'I've been taking care of my mother for quite a while now, Neve,' Portia said levelly. 'Believe me, she needs it. That's why it was such a relief to have Rob take over, I can tell you.'

Neve blinked at her but Portia was in deadly earnest.

'Uh, look, let's sit down and I'll get us... something.'

'Great. By the way, I also brought one of my stories over to show you.' Portia sat in the same chair her father had two days ago and opened her bag.

Whereas Neve, feeling as if she should pinch herself, escaped to the kitchen. What on earth should she do, she wondered frantically. Well, there was no question of what she should do, but how could she stem the flow of confidences the child was so ready to bestow upon her?

Five minutes later she took two glasses of pine-apple juice and a plate of buttered gingerbread into the lounge.

'Yummy! Thanks,' Portia said enthusiastically. 'So—'

'Portia.' Neve sat down. 'Before we go any fur-ther, I feel I have to say this. Your parents would be aghast not only if they knew you were here instead of at your drama class— How did you get here by the way?'

'Took a cab with my pocket money,' Portia said nonchalantly.

'OK. But they would also be horrified to think that you were spilling all the family secrets to a relative stranger.'

'Well, that's one thing I heard Rob say to Mum— the only two people who didn't know the secret were he and I! Apparently the whole world knew I was his daughter.'

Neve decided not to comment on this. 'Couldn't you have gone to…someone else? Close to the fam-ily, I mean?'

'I wanted an unbiased opinion, Neve,' Portia said stubbornly. 'I once heard Mum say to Rob—I haven't got used to calling him Dad yet!—anyway, I once heard her say your brand of journalism was the most unbiased she'd read for a long time. And you're not a stranger.'

'But what about Toni or Bill and Bunny or your grandparents?'

'My grandparents live in Townsville but I just wanted to talk it over with you, Neve.' Portia looked distinctly mutinous. 'That's the other thing Mum said, how well you must have understood Rob to write the article you did.'

Neve flinched inwardly.

'But the thing is,' Portia went on, 'they don't have to get married because of me.'

Shock widened Neve's eyes. '...They don't?' she said feebly.

'Of course not! No one can take Rob away from me now, and if you've got to *argue* about getting married, how many arguments are you going to have when you do get married?'

The logic of this, to a child anyway, must seem inescapable, Neve mused silently and sighed. 'So you'd be quite happy for them to go on as before? But they were getting married anyway.'

'Well, I didn't think it was a very good idea,' Portia said flatly. 'Mum needs people to need her. Otherwise she feels—there's a word for it but I can't think of it.'

'Inadequate?' Neve suggested. 'But you just said it was such a relief to have Rob looking after her.'

'Yes—but she really felt needed so it didn't look as if Rob was looking after her! Now Rob's over the worst, he's not going to need her as he has, so...' She shrugged.

'But you must enjoy having them in the same house with you, especially now?'

'Not if they're going to fight all the time.'

'Portia, they won't,' Neve said gently. 'This must have come as a big surprise, it's natural that things are a bit turbulent—'

'That's the other thing,' Portia said glumly, 'I don't want to have to take sides—'

'You don't have to do that.'

'But why did she keep it as a secret? Why didn't she even tell me?'

'Perhaps she hasn't had a chance to explain things to you yet. Portia, I'm going to ring them now. I must.' Neve stood up.

'So what do you think I should do, Neve?'

'Let them work it out,' Neve advised. Then she couldn't help herself, she went over and gave Portia a hug. The child responded gratefully.

'But until they get here, I would love to read your story,' Neve added.

She got Rob on the phone as she knew she would—fate, luck or whatever hadn't been on her side since she'd met Rob Stowe.

'Neve?' he said incredulously down the line.

'Yes, Rob, I'm just ringing to let you know that Portia is here with me.'

There was a thunderstruck silence on the other end of the line, then, 'What the hell are you talking about?'

Neve swallowed and tried to explain as calmly as possible.

'But why?' he asked incredulously.

Neve lowered her voice, she was making the call from her bedroom extension, and tried to explain further, briefly.

'You're joking,' he said flatly.

'Believe me I am not and if you think for one minute I lured her here—'

'I didn't say that—'

'Will you come and fetch her?' Neve broke in.

'I've sent Jeff and the car home and Molly is out—

she was going to pick Portia up—Neve, could you bring her home in a taxi? I'll ring the drama class and tell them to tell Molly there's nothing to be frantic about. Will you?'

'I...oh, all right.'

'Thanks. See you soon,' he said briefly and put the phone down.

For once in her life, Portia looked faintly apprehensive as they walked up to the burgundy front door.

But it was Rob himself who opened it and Rob who said, 'Portia, don't you dare do anything like that again! Now I'm your father I can not only tell you what to do and what not to do, but I can also get grey hairs over you.'

But he was reaching for her as he spoke and they clung together.

Neve backed away silently. She'd asked the taxi to wait and told Portia that she would go back in it. The child had protested but she'd said that this was between her and her dad and mum now, and any good journalist knew when to fade into the background.

On Friday afternoon, Rob Stowe leant against the mudguard of his Range Rover and watched as Neve came out of the building she worked in.

She stopped on the bottom step, patted her purse as if she was in two minds about having forgotten something, then she looked up at the building in a rueful sort of way.

It was warm again and she wore a short beige linen sleeveless dress, sheer stockings on her long legs and smart brown suede shoes. Her hair was gathered back in a bright saffron bow and although she looked essentially chic, she also looked pale and tired, he thought.

He watched for a moment longer as she started to walk away with her long-legged stride and wondered why one woman's walk should have the effect it did on him. Then he straightened, followed her and tapped her on the shoulder.

She turned convulsively and dropped her purse when she saw who it was. Fortunately it didn't spill open but there was a little flush in her cheeks as she bent to retrieve it and said, 'I don't know why fate always seems to put us in each other's path—'

'Not fate this time, Neve,' he interrupted.

She straightened with a wary look in her violet eyes. 'What do you mean? Have you...what have you done?'

He shrugged. 'Nothing, but I'm taking you out to dinner.'

'No...' She swallowed something in her throat. 'Thank you very much but I...that is to say...'

'Surely we can be friends,' he murmured. 'That's what you decided you felt for me, didn't you?' His dark eyes were slightly ironic. 'So it's not as if it would be painful for you or anything like that, now would it?'

'I...' She gazed at him helplessly. He wore a charcoal suit and a pale grey shirt with a green and blue striped tie.

'If you're worried about me, I'm a lot tougher than I look,' he said with a quirk of humour in his eyes.

'I...'

He waited a moment but she couldn't go on. He said a little dryly, 'We're creating a bit of a traffic jam, Neve. It is five o'clock and people are starting to stream home.'

She looked around to see that they were creating a small island in a sea of people, and he put a hand on her arm and led her to the Range Rover.

'So you can drive now,' she said foolishly as he got into the driver's seat.

'As you see. Before long I'll be able to dance.'

'How about riding, whitewater rafting and so on?'

'No. Don't think I'll risk it.' He steered the Range Rover out into the traffic. 'By the way, I wanted to say thank you for handling Portia so well.'

'I didn't do much at all. I got such a surprise.'

He glanced at her. 'She admires you tremendously.'

'Young girls do tend to…pick role models, I suppose. I'm sure it won't last. Someone else will come along.'

He didn't comment on that. 'I believe you're on holiday?'

'Who told you that?'

'George.'

'How did you come to be discussing me with George?' she asked frostily.

'Can't remember,' he drawled. 'But I believe Brent is back and dying to get into the swing of things.'

Neve stared at him levelly but he simply drove on unconcernedly. 'Yes, I am on holiday,' she said at last.

'Got anything planned?'

'Yes.'

His lips twisted. 'You're very uncommunicative, Neve.'

'I'm not sure what I'm doing here with you let alone discussing any plans I have with you—it could be that,' she elucidated.

'Or it could be that you don't have any,' he shot back.

'Rob,' she said wearily, 'it's got nothing to do with you how I live my life, but as a matter of fact, I have. I've booked a holiday unit at Byron Bay, I go up by train tomorrow and return the following Sunday. I plan to soak up the sun, swim, walk and relax.'

'Alone?'

'Yes,' she said dangerously. 'Please don't make anything of it, I feel like being alone...' She stopped abruptly and bit her lip.

'We're here,' he said quietly.

Neve looked out of the window as he pulled up in front of a very famous fish restaurant at Watson's Bay. 'Isn't it too early for dinner?'

'Not really. We can have a drink first, soak up the last of this lovely sunny Sydney day then eat leisurely.'

Neve looked out at the beach beyond the terrace of the restaurant, at the boats on the harbour and the diamonds the setting sun was creating on the water. 'OK,' she said, helplessly again.

They didn't talk at all until he'd ordered a beer for himself and a gin and tonic for her. Then he said, 'You may not believe this, but I was extremely grateful for the things you said to Portia. And extremely mortified to think of what Molly and I had put her through.'

Neve glanced at him through her lashes. 'She may not have been meant to overhear the things you said.'

'What kid wouldn't be tempted to listen at doors?'

Neve smiled faintly. 'I wouldn't blame yourself too much.'

'But I do,' he said harshly. 'I handled the whole thing so badly. Well, not at first.' He looked thoughtful. 'I took Molly aside when they got home from the fête and told her what had happened. She was horrified then intensely relieved and she started to cry and Portia came in and asked what was going on so we told her.'

He paused and looked out over the harbour, then said, 'In the joyfulness of that moment, I truly thought everything would take care of itself, which just goes to show how naive you can be.'

'When did you all start to tumble down from cloud nine?' Neve asked quietly.

'The very next day. Molly took it into her head to tell me that she now felt as if she was forcing me to marry her and it didn't sit easily with her. I lost my temper and told her she'd never had a better reason to marry me, but what the hell had she thought she was doing hiding it from me for so long and did she realize what a fool she'd made of me?' He grimaced.

'I guess it was inevitable—to come back to earth, I mean. I hope you persuaded her that once you'd got it off your chest you—'

'No, I wasn't able to persuade her,' he broke in. 'For one thing, when Molly sets a course in her mind, very little can change it. For another, she was devastated to think of Portia being upset. And thirdly, when Portia gave it as her considered opinion that we shouldn't marry, Molly—upped stakes.'

Neve stared at him wide-eyed. 'You mean... walked out?'

He nodded. 'But only back to her parents in Townsville, it's not as if she's run off with Portia.'

'Thank heavens!' Neve breathed relievedly. 'But you really shouldn't have—I mean she's only twelve, she's so thrilled to know you're her father and she's...*she's* horrified at the thought of having to take sides.'

He looked at her sombrely.

'I'm sorry,' she said after a moment. 'It's so easy to sound righteous when you're not involved.' She sighed and sipped her drink. 'Actually, it all sounds very human and the kinds of things families are prone to.'

'It doesn't make it any less difficult...' He stopped and shrugged. 'But one thing has come out of it, and it has nothing whatsoever to do with you, Neve.'

'I'm glad,' she said barely audibly.

'You don't know what I'm going to say.' He eyed her.

'Whatever it is, there's no place for me in any of this, Rob. I thought we'd sorted that out.'

He leant back in his chair and studied the amber liquid in his glass. 'Do you mean—' he raised his dark eyes to hers and they were supremely sardonic '—when you gave me to understand that you didn't fancy me in the slightest?'

Neve choked on a sip of gin and tonic. She put the glass down and with her eyes watering, spluttered, 'I...I...'

'Neve, Neve,' he marvelled. 'You're not usually lost for a word. It's your career, isn't it? Nor are you usually less than adept at responding to a right jab with a left hook.'

'All right, go on,' she said with more spirit.

He smiled lethally and played with his coaster in his long fingers. 'You also gave me to understand,' he said reminiscently, 'that I was a dangerously frustrated man who was very much afraid he might not be capable of making love to a woman—did I get that bit right?'

'So?'

'I just wanted to be sure that's how we'd worked things out, that's all. Or rather, you did.'

She was silent, breathing a little raggedly and unsure where all this was leading, as her violet eyes demonstrated.

But he drained his beer and put the glass down precisely in the centre of the coaster before he continued. 'I wanted to be sure so that when I tell you that I now know I could no more marry and live with Molly Condren than I could fly, you won't be tempted to think *you've* come between us, Neve Williams.'

CHAPTER SIX

'You're joking!' Neve said incredulously.

'No, I'm not.' He raised an eyebrow at her and added dryly, 'Would I joke about something like that?'

'But why?' she said hoarsely.

'We wouldn't suit.'

'You suited fine for two years,' she protested.

'This is different—' He broke off as the waiter came to take their order. 'Do try the lobster, Neve,' he suggested, 'and how about some oysters to start?'

'I hate oysters,' Neve said flatly, causing both Rob Stowe and the waiter to look amused.

'May I suggest the calamari then, ma'am?' the waiter murmured. 'It's very fresh.'

'Calamari is tasteless and rubbery to my palate, I'm afraid.'

'Perhaps I brought you to the wrong restaurant?' Rob drawled. 'Unless you're being deliberately re-calcitrant?'

She raised her violet eyes to his and they were furious. But before she could open her mouth to say anything, he grinned and sheer devilry glinted in his eyes. 'That's more my Neve—have you anything against a small Caesar salad? They do it very well here with anchovies, sliced parmesan, real bacon not rubbery bits of—'

'Yes, thank you, that will do fine. And I'll have the John Dory fillets in a light batter.' She closed the menu decisively and picked up her drink. But her eyes were still stormy as she stared out over the water.

'What are we fighting about?' Rob remarked after a pause. He had ordered oysters and lobster, and a bottle of wine.

'Your bloody-mindedness at times,' she rejoined with something of a snap.

'Ah. I apologize for calling you recalcitrant—'

'You'd be better advised to stop and think before you say these things.'

'Yes, ma'am, sorry, ma'am,' he said meekly.

'And don't think that fools me for a moment, either!'

'What would you like me to do?' he inquired wryly.

'Stop fooling around and *tell* me why you won't marry Molly!'

He took his time. He studied her for a long moment then he shrugged. 'I would drive her mad and she would drive me mad, Neve. It's as simple as that. You yourself have just told me how bloody-minded I can be.'

'But you must have realized this before... before...' She stopped frustratedly.

'No, not really. It took the full force of her foolishness in certain respects to bring it home to me, you see. Now, I'm quite sure there is a man out there who could balance all the rash things she does with all her wonderful qualities and love the whole, but it's not me.'

'A man,' Neve said slowly, 'who would be Portia's stepfather.'

'Perhaps,' he conceded with a nerve flickering in

his jaw. 'But I know myself well enough now to know that I would make Molly's life a nightmare.'

'What Portia would really like is for your lives to go on as it has been.' Neve made a little gesture.

'But it can't,' he said slowly. 'And Portia—there's no way we can lose each other now even if we can't live together all the time as a family.'

'She said that, too,' Neve murmured involuntarily but added immediately, 'You'd miss her.'

'Do you think I don't know that?' His gaze was suddenly harsh. 'But at least the time I have with her will be happy and peaceful.'

'All right,' Neve said at last. 'It's your decision. I can't approve but...' She shrugged.

'Are these your puritan instincts coming to the fore?' he asked cynically.

She looked at him through her lashes then away. 'Possibly.'

'And how would they affect us?'

'Us?' She blinked at him—and the waiter delivered their first courses.

'Yes, us,' Rob Stowe said when they were alone again, Neve confronting a Caesar salad and he a platter of oysters Kilpatrick. 'You and I, Neve Williams, journalist and Rob Stowe—'

'Don't start again!' she warned tightly.

'Well, I didn't think you were obtuse, Neve,' he said impatiently.

'You...you told me this had nothing whatsoever to do with me,' she protested. 'Amongst other things,' she added swiftly.

He smiled coolly. 'Ah, those other things,' he murmured. 'We'll get to them. But the rest of it *doesn't* have anything to do with you. And perhaps you should bear in mind that *you* told me that to marry a woman out of gratitude was a recipe for disaster.'

Neve swallowed a crouton and a bit of bacon and reached for the glass of wine that had materialized in front of her. 'That was before…that was…'

'Before *I* knew about Portia?'

'…Yes.'

'But not the rest of the world,' he said dryly.

'That obviously irks you, Rob, and I can understand why,' she said quietly, 'but it's trivial really.'

He pushed his oyster platter away. 'This isn't, however. I have not the slightest desire to make love to Molly although I'll *always* love her in a way, and always be grateful to her. But it took a—combination of things to make me realize that the greatest disservice I could do to her, would be to marry her. Now—' he fiddled with the stem of his wineglass and continued almost clinically, 'I told you that had nothing to do with you.'

'Yes,' Neve agreed a little pointedly.

He looked at her ruefully but went on. 'You're not the reason I can't make myself love Molly properly, although you are one of the reasons I've been able to see it at last. But the real reason I can't do it has another name—Portia.'

'I would have thought—'

'So did I at first. The best reason in the world to do it. But we would only end up tearing Portia apart—as my friends could have told me apparently,' he said a shade darkly, then grimaced. 'People who do know me when I'm…normal, though. As in health-wise.'

A fleeting look of humour came to his eyes and

he waited for a moment as if to give her time to contest this.

She said nothing.

'So it is a separate issue, Neve, the fact that if I could take you somewhere private now, and if we were to kiss each other as we did once before, it would take an almost inhuman effort of will, not to make love to you.'

'You...' She licked her lips. 'You don't believe what I told you?'

'No. Well, at the time I was suitably crushed. And I was furious to think that a slip of a girl—' his gaze roamed over her '—nearly ten years younger than me could demolish me so effectively. And I am, heaven help me...' He paused, looking grim.

Neve found she was holding her breath.

'I am as bloody nervous about taking this particular step as if I were a virgin myself,' he said with his own brand of painful honesty that she'd so admired when she'd finally got him to talk about himself during the interview. 'But the only woman in the world I want to try it with, happens to be you.'

Her eyes softened.

He sat back looking suddenly exhausted. 'Would it be too much to hope that you did it, *said* what you did—because of your scruples, your morals, your concern for Portia and Molly and no other reason, Neve?'

She suddenly realized that her Caesar salad had gone and a plate of golden John Dory fillets in batter sat before her.

'Neve?'

'Rob, no, it wouldn't be too much to hope,' she

answered barely audibly. 'I was intensely affected by you, too. But—'

'Don't,' he said. 'This may be a very wounded ego talking but could I just savour the moment?'

They gazed at each other and she could see the sudden hunger in his eyes as they ranged over her, and feel a corresponding rush of desire surge through her veins. It was as if they were alone on the planet and it was the most intensely physical sensation that had ever come to her without even being touched by a man.

So much so that her cheeks reddened and she moved abruptly in bewilderment and shock.

'Eat, Neve,' he said gently. 'But don't for one moment imagine that you're alone in feeling like this.'

She picked up her knife and fork distractedly but didn't begin to eat. 'It's never happened to me before.'

He smiled faintly. 'I have to say I'm glad.'

A moment of humour came to her. 'I'd hate to think what you could do to me if I was in your arms.'

He stared at her wordlessly then said simply, 'Thanks.'

'But—'

'You told me once that it made you very happy to know that I desired you. What you just said has done the same for me.'

Neve did start to eat. And as she did, she examined all sorts of new phenomena. How unusually delicious her fish fillets were, how exquisite the sunset was. How she couldn't think of anywhere on earth she'd rather be but sitting on a terrace beside the beach with this man. How happy she was that she'd worn one of her favourite dresses to work that morning...

'Could I come to Byron Bay with you?'

Her lashes lifted abruptly and she gazed at him wide-eyed.

He looked rueful. 'Did *I* break the moment?'

'No. No…well…' She swallowed. 'I *hadn't* thought beyond it yet.'

'I couldn't tell what you were thinking—sometimes I can, mostly when you're laughing at me but at other times it's as if you can conceal your innermost thoughts with an impenetrable reserve and that's part of the fascination.'

She sipped some wine. 'I was just—amazed at how everything—tasted better, looked better, felt better.'

'It could be the same at Byron Bay,' he said quietly.

'Rob—for the whole week?'

'Maybe not. I have to go up to Townsville—' He broke off and slid his hand across the table to cover hers. 'You do understand, don't you, Neve?'

'I…' She paused and felt some of the enchantment of the moment fade. 'I can't think straight to be honest, Rob. But I do know it would upset me to think…to think of Molly and Portia on their own and you and I…' She stopped confusedly.

'Happy and in love?' he supplied.

'Well, yes. It's so soon.' She sighed.

He thought for a moment, then, 'Could I come to Byron Bay to tell you how things have been settled?'

'Do you mean—'

'I mean, no pressure to sleep with me unless you're happy to.'

Their eyes locked. 'It has come to that, hasn't it, Neve?' he queried.

She was silent.

'As well as to decide if you're going to marry me.'

Still she was silent.

'Because we can't work any of those things out unless we're together,' he added.

'...You're right,' she said at last.

'Then in the meantime, should we do one of the two things we do best—so far, that is?' A glint of devilry lit his dark eyes.

'You'll have to be more specific, Rob,' she said gravely.

He sat back looking relieved. 'You're laughing at me again, Neve Williams. Uh—specific? Well, we kiss really well, specifically. We also talk together well, and seeing this is a rather public spot—' he looked around wryly '—I think we should opt for that.'

A gurgle of laughter rose in her throat. 'I'd love to.'

So they did. Until about nine o'clock. Unspecific talk, in that they made no mention of their feelings for each other but the knowledge was there, just under the surface.

'I think I better take you home,' he said at last. 'What time does your train go in the morning?'

She told him and they left soon afterwards. To drive home slowly. 'Can I take you to the station?' he asked. 'You don't seem to drive.'

'I do. I was driving tractors almost before I could walk, but I don't have a car in Sydney.'

He pulled up in front of her block of units. 'So. May I?'

'If you like,' she said softly. 'Would you...would you like to come up?'

'I'd love to but—it might not be a good idea. Well, not tonight.'

'I think I know what you mean,' she said softly as they couldn't seem to tear their eyes from each other.

'Which is not to say I can't do this.' He put an arm around her shoulders and their mouths rested lightly together then they drew apart, laughed and hugged each other.

'I think I better go,' she teased. 'I think you better. See you tomorrow!'

She found it hard to sleep that night.

Not only because of the way he'd kissed her goodnight, a way that had left her trembling and aroused, but because, of course, of the momentous decisions that lay ahead of her.

She had a bath when she got home and finished her packing, then she put some music on the CD player, made herself a cup of coffee and curled up on the settee. And as John Williams played his classical guitar, two words seemed to print themselves on her mind—Neve Stowe.

A wife, living in Woollahra, no longer a career girl, married to a man she barely knew. Stepmother to Portia—that would be nice but... She sighed suddenly. It was true, he was a man she barely knew much as she might be physically affected by him. But physical attractions notoriously didn't take into account such things as lifestyle expectations, how he would feel about her working, for example, how she would feel about becoming a mother.

On the other hand, she mused, she'd felt dreadful when she'd sent him back to Molly.

So, did love take care of all those things? Or was it wiser to have a relationship with a man before you made a decision?

She had to smile to herself although painfully, because this went so against the grain of her upbringing, it was hard to believe she could think it. But the thing was, she thought then, how hard was it going to be not to sleep with him while she did get to know him better? And then there was the spectre of Molly Condren—did she really love Rob Stowe?

She eventually took herself to bed with nothing resolved but filled with a longing for the magic of being with him. Was she just too cautious, she wondered. Was that why her life *was* pretty solitary—or she had unwittingly allowed it to get that way, at least?

He was even able to carry her bag on to the train for her the next morning.

Prompting her to say, as they sat in the compartment with about ten minutes to spare, 'Rob, you've improved so dramatically over the last two months, it's amazing.'

'I know. I think it's something to do with—well, two things. All the work on those muscles that had lain idle finally takes effect. And once you can take one small step, it's a hell of an incentive.'

'Are you in pain at all now?'

He grimaced. 'Sometimes. My own fault, though, when I overdo things. As a matter of fact that was why I was back in the chair when we first met, I tore a muscle lifting weights and set myself back a good few weeks—by the way, these are for you.' He handed her a carrier bag.

She opened it to find fruit, chocolates and a selection of magazines. She was so touched she leaned across and kissed him lightly. 'Thank you.'

They held hands for a moment then she dragged her mind unwillingly from the physical sensations filling her just to be sitting opposite him holding hands. 'Uh—so you had been walking before then?'

He let her hand go and sat back looking wry. 'Yep. Not that easily, but I had.'

'Maybe that's why you were in such a bad mood that first day?' she suggested with a grin.

A smile lit his dark eyes. 'I certainly didn't appreciate being chair-bound in front of a tall, slim girl who alternately laughed at me and told me to do my damnedest. You know, Neve, there's something about the way you walk that compounded my—blues with that bloody wheelchair.'

She looked surprised. 'I don't think I walk any differently from any other girl.'

'Oh, yes, you do,' he contradicted. 'And I've had many a long dark night to wonder about it. Like to know what conclusion I came to?'

'Well, yes, if it's a complimentary conclusion.'

He grinned. 'Anything about the way you walk that can keep a man awake and in torment at night has to be complimentary!'

'Tell me,' she invited.

'The thing is, you don't teeter, you don't take short steps, you have a lovely fluid stride that is a joy to behold especially from behind—and my theory on it is that it comes from having five brothers and playing rugby with them.'

Neve blinked then started to laugh.

'It's no laughing matter.' He looked pained. 'You perceive a man desperately short of sleep!'

'I wasn't laughing about that. Having a rugby-playing stride doesn't sound essentially feminine to me, that's all.' But she was still laughing.

'Believe me, it's wonderful,' he said simply.

She sobered at last and once again, as they stared at each other, they were caught in the grip of their desire for each other.

'I think we're about to go,' she said at last.

'I think you're right.' He stood up. 'Look after yourself, Neve Williams.'

'I will. You, too!' But they stared at each other for a long moment, before he finally stepped off the train.

And she waved foolishly from the window even when she could no longer see him.

She had three days at Byron Bay on her own.

Lovely days with beautiful sunny weather, wonderful swimming conditions and nothing to do but please herself. The holiday apartment she'd rented was just across the road from the beach and the beach at Byron Bay was something special.

Protected from the prevailing south-easterlies by the bulk of Cape Byron, the most easterly point of Australia, and protected as few other beaches on the east coast are, it was a haven of warmth and blue water. Julian Rocks, out in the bay, shimmered, on those three days, in a glittering blue sea.

She walked for miles, along the beach, up the path to the lighthouse with its sheer drop on the other side of the headland down to the sea. She even spotted a whale making its northward migration to the warmer waters of Hervey Bay in Queensland to spawn.

Byron was also a hive of little restaurants and home to a laid-back community with an alternative lifestyle flavour. For years it had resisted high-rise development so although it was very much a holiday town, it was also quaint with some strange people in strange garb wandering around yet still delightful.

She wondered once what the mega-rich might make of it although Paul Hogan of *Crocodile Dundee* fame and his partner John Cornell had homes in the area. But she wondered specifically about the man she was expecting. Because Byron Bay was not essentially sophisticated.

Then he was on her doorstep, having rung her on her mobile to tell her when to expect him. On her doorstep in khaki shorts, loafers and a green T-shirt and looking like a Rob Stowe she had never seen, younger and light-hearted. He had no luggage but the first thing he said set her mind to rest on one score.

He said with a grin, 'Don't know why but Byron always does this to me, makes me feel good.'

She sighed with relief then he took her in his arms and added, 'But not nearly as good as being able to do this does.'

'How are you? How are they?' she asked sometime later after they'd kissed with a passionate intensity that had made her dizzy again. And he'd been the one to suggest they have a drink and produced a bottle of wine in a brown paper packet.

They were out on the veranda of the apartment, watching the sun set. Neve wore a pair of denim shorts with a blue knit top over her bikini and had her pink sand shoes on.

He set the two glasses of wine on the table between them and eased himself into a lounger.

'Things have happened,' he said slowly. 'Molly gave me to understand as soon as I arrived that she hadn't changed her mind, she wouldn't feel right about marrying me now—this was before I had a chance to say anything—and anyway, she's been offered the star role in a television series and she's accepted.'

'That's...' But Neve was lost for words.

'That's the way things can happen with Molly, Neve,' he said slowly and grimaced. 'Even I'd forgotten how, all those years ago, she was with me one day then gone the next.'

'You don't think it's her way of coping with loving you but...perhaps knowing you don't love her?'

He looked at her steadily. 'I'll tell you what else she said—she said that as soon as we'd started to argue, she'd realized she'd conned herself into believing, for Portia's sake, that I had changed and that I still needed her. She told me that one of the reasons she'd left me in the first place, all those years ago, was because I *didn't* need her and I'd had a way of dominating her—'

Neve made a small sound.

He looked at her sombrely. 'Not physically, but in imposing my...way of doing things on her, she said. It made her feel mentally flattened, she said. And she suggested that whoever I did marry would need the particular strength of character she'd lacked, to cope with me.'

'Did you feel that at the time?' Neve asked with a frown.

'I...' He paused and looked out to sea. 'I am renowned, as my friends didn't hesitate to tell *you* one day, for walking all over people. But no, I didn't realize that's what I was doing to Molly. I seem to think you and I won't have that problem, though.'

He looked back at her and a curious sensation came over Neve during the long, sober gaze they exchanged, making her aware that in any kind of a relationship with this man, there would always be times when they would clash...

'If you're thinking what I'm thinking,' he said barely audibly.

'That I'll resist being walked all over to the bitter end?' she murmured.

'Precisely.'

'It doesn't sound like a recipe for...ease and comfort.' She raised an eyebrow at him.

'But then, we're not talking about slippers. We're talking about the fact that an integral part of how we affect each other, is to do with our independence, intellectual and otherwise, wouldn't you agree?'

She stared at him steadily. 'Can you combine the two? Marriage and independence of whatever kind?'

'I think so. I think it will provide the grounds for us never to get bored with each other.'

Neve looked away at last. 'So—what other plans do Molly and Portia have?'

He sat back. 'This TV series is being shot on the south coast of New South Wales. For the next three months Molly will be on location there during the week and back in Sydney for the weekends. Portia will stay with me during the week.' He paused. 'I'm going to buy Molly a house as close to mine as I can find so that Portia will be able come and go between us easily.'

'That still doesn't tell me anything about their state of mind,' Neve said slowly.

'Then perhaps this will. It's as if a great weight has been lifted from all of us. Molly is as excited as a child about getting back before the cameras. She and I are back on our old footing, always friends but able to laugh together now, and Portia is intensely relieved.'

Neve blinked away some tears. 'Are you sure?'

'Neve,' he said deliberately, 'do you honestly think I wouldn't do absolutely all in my power to take care of these two people who mean so much to me in one way or another?'

'No, I don't believe...that.'

'Then—will you marry me?'

Her violet eyes jerked to his. 'Rob, I...I...don't know yet,' she stammered.

He smiled suddenly. 'I wasn't going to do that, you know. Many a horse has come a cropper from rushing its fences but—for the record, don't forget I said it. By the way, I booked into the Byron Bay Hotel.'

Confusion lit her eyes. 'I wondered why you had no luggage. I...'

'Thought I ought to make good my promise of no pressure,' he said wryly. 'Like to have a wander down to the beach?'

'Yes, I mean, if you're up to it. I...' Again she stopped uncertainly.

His eyes softened. 'Finish your drink, Neve,' he advised. 'Then we'll take a gentle stroll and let time just take care of us in the meanwhile.'

They walked and sat on the beach until darkness fell. Then they strolled into town and bought fish and chips and went back to the beach to sit on the sand against a grassy bank and eat their supper with their fingers.

'I'm looking forward to a swim tomorrow,' Rob said idly.

'The water has been superb. Byron at its best,' Neve murmured. 'What we should do is have an early swim tomorrow, the tide is good then, and have breakfast at that café at Clark's Beach.' She stopped and listened to the rhythmic crash of the surf on the beach and sniffed the salty air appreciatively.

'You're on. What time is early?'

'Six o'clock?'

He groaned. 'Don't tell me you're an early bird, Miss Williams?'

'You forget, I grew up in the country,' she said primly.

'Up at dawn kind of thing.' He grimaced. 'Don't tell me you're an early to bed type, too!'

'I do like my sleep.' This time she sounded virtuous.

He swore softly beneath his breath.

'I gather you're the opposite?' she said seriously.

'You gather right, a real night owl.' He rolled their fish and chip papers into a neat ball, and taking her with him, leant back against the bank of grass. 'We'll need to make some adjustments,' he said against her cheek as he cradled her in his arms.

'I don't go to bed that early,' Neve replied, relenting.

'I know that,' he responded. 'You were teasing me.'

'Not about early morning swims, I wasn't,' she

denied and relaxed against him. 'Look at the stars,' she added dreamily. 'You know, I wasn't looking forward to this holiday but, if nothing else, I've thought a lot about...me.' She grimaced.

He kissed her cheek. 'And what did you decide?'

'One of the problems of being a journalist is, well, *can* be, that you tend to become an observer, not a participant.'

'Do you think that's what's happened to you?'

'I'm wondering. I think I may also have been born cautious by nature.'

'You don't kiss me cautiously.'

'You...may just be a hard person *to* kiss cautiously, Rob Stowe!'

'I know I have a few reputations but that hasn't been one of them.'

'Really? There must have been other women in your life apart from Molly.'

'There have been.' She felt him shrug. 'None that I've asked to marry me, however. And, while I may not have lived like a monk, I'm not a womaniser.'

'That's easy to say.'

He gathered her closer. 'Neve, I'm strictly a one-woman-at-a-time man, there were two relationships that lasted some time and both times I thought I was in love. It turned out not to be the case.'

'I see.'

'I know what you're going to ask me next,' he said gravely. 'How can I know I'm in love with you then?'

Neve thought for a bit. 'You're not offended by these questions?'

'Nope.'

'Why not?' she asked, still staring up at the stars.

'Because I'm about to prove several things to you. A—you're shortly to become very much a participant. B—you're also about to become the exact opposite of cautious and C—so am I. And I think all these things may speak for themselves.'

'Oh.'

'Any further objections?' he asked wickedly.

A slight tremor ran down her body as his hands moved on her.

'After all, this is a public beach,' he murmured.

She tensed but partly because that hadn't even crossed her mind and he started to laugh softly in the moment before he began to kiss her.

'You're…impossible,' she did manage to say.

'I know. But you're impossibly beautiful and desirable to me, Neve. If you must blame anything, blame that.'

It went further, this kiss, than any of his others. He slid his hands beneath her blue knit top and unclasped her bikini top. The feel of his hands on her breasts was powerfully arousing and sent quivers of sensation through her. She buried her head in his shoulder and breathed raggedly but when he immediately withdrew his hands she whispered, 'No, don't stop.'

'It's not that I want to, I didn't want to hurt you, that's all.'

'I'm not sure that you aren't,' she gasped as her nipples peaked beneath his fingers. 'No, I mean, you're not, it's just that it's so—' She broke off and bit her lip.

'I know what you mean—how to go no further?'

'Yes,' she breathed and added helplessly, 'I had a feeling this would happen to me.'

He did withdraw his hands and he pulled her into his arms again, and waited until her breathing had steadied before he said, with an effort, 'One small step at a time. If anyone should know that, I should.'

She lay against him, feeling suddenly warm and cherished and with her heart beating with sheer love for him. Almost to the point, she realized with a jolt, of saying, *Yes, Rob, I will marry you...*

And the shock of it made her go suddenly rigid in his arms.

'What?' He leant up on one elbow and looked down at her at the same time as he played with a strand of her hair.

'I...nothing.'

'Neve,' he said quietly but insistently.

She sat up and brushed herself down and he made no move to stop her. 'This is...this,' she said at last. 'But it's not the sometimes deadly, daily routine of living together. It doesn't tell me how you would cope with the fact that I may never want to give up my career. Or how I would cope with Rob Stowe, millionaire businessman.'

He went to say something but she stopped him with her fingers gently against his mouth. 'Let me finish. If I take any step now, I think it would have to be a relationship. I never thought I would or could but, I just don't know you well enough, Rob, to plunge into marriage.'

'That's a pity,' he said after an age. 'Because— I'm only prepared to do this the right and proper way.'

'What?' She stared at him stunned.

His lips twisted. 'Bit of role reversal, I agree. But, well, that's it.'

She tried to speak a couple of times but nothing came out.

'You're amazed?' he suggested with some irony.

She said something uncomplimentary beneath her breath and he grinned fleetingly.

He also said, 'Women obviously regard that particular ultimatum as their prerogative.'

Neve choked this time on a combination of disbelief and ire.

He patted her on the back obligingly.

'Don't,' she warned, regaining some composure. And when he looked at her inquiringly, she added angrily, 'Joke about it, patronise me or pat me on the back. *Why!*'

His gaze was suddenly steady. 'That's the way I feel about you, Neve Williams. As simple as that.'

'It can't possibly be…simple. We barely—'

'Barely know each other,' he parodied. 'I certainly know enough to know what I want to do. I know you're beautiful, unusually mature, that you ignite me and I'm miserable—and hell to live with—without you. And, dear Neve,' he said, 'what do you think a relationship is going to throw up? Surely we can overcome the little things like who leaves the lid off the toothpaste or squeezes the tube from the top?'

Once again she stared at him speechlessly.

'Whereas,' he went on solemnly, 'any other major differences should still surface before we tie the knot and sleep with each other—you don't seriously think there's going to be a problem with that, do you? Or are you still worried about my abilities in that regard?'

'No,' she said hastily. 'Oh, hell! I can't believe I'm having this conversation with you.'

'It is normally held the other way around, as I pointed out before,' he said softly but with such a wealth of ironic amusement, she flinched visibly.

He waited.

'So,' she said at last, 'your ultimatum to me is, marry me or…let's leave it at that?'

'Something like that,' he murmured. 'I don't expect you to rush to the altar with me tomorrow or—'

'This is a change of heart, Rob,' she interrupted. 'Only four nights ago, next to another beach, you said something to me about—*it has come to that, hasn't it, Neve?* In relation to us sleeping together, Rob,' she added warningly, so there could be no misunderstanding.

He smiled, and leant forward to kiss her lightly on the lips. 'I'm a wiser man, now, Neve. That's all.'

'But why? I still don't understand.'

'You should. It's the way you would, in your heart of hearts, rather do it.'

She stared at him wordlessly. And in the light of all the stars above them, she could see nothing amused or patronising or ironic in his eyes now.

He said then, 'You may like to think you barely know me, Neve. But there are things I know instinctively about you. Just as there are things I've told you about me I hadn't ever intended to tell a soul. That's what's between us.'

'I…' She shook her head as if to clear it.

But he stood up and held his hand out to her. And when she got to her feet, he said, 'Think about it. In the meantime, I'm going to walk you to your door then retire to my hotel.'

He started to walk with her hand in his. And along the way, as they wove their way beneath the giant hoop pines that lined the beach and scrunched pine needles beneath their feet, he said, 'I've got some of Portia's creative genius with me. She asked me if I could show them to you. Did you realize what a floodgate you opened when you gave her the advice you did?'

Neve grimaced. 'No. But I'm glad. And she's very good for a twelve-year-old.' She stopped walking. 'She doesn't know about us—that you're here and—'

'No. No one does, yet. She thought I might see you in Sydney.'

'Oh.'

'We're here,' he said quietly, and gestured across the road to her holiday unit. 'Is this a good place to meet you at six o'clock tomorrow morning?'

'Uh…yes, but we could make it seven if you like,' Neve answered a bit dazedly.

'I don't think getting up early is going to be a problem, tomorrow.' He looked at her gravely.

'You're the one—' Neve stopped as his hand tightened on hers briefly.

'Tell me this honestly, Neve. Would you have slept with me tonight?'

'I don't know. In sound mind I may not have,' she said huskily. 'But then, as you know, I can sometimes throw caution to the winds.'

They were standing beneath a streetlight so they could see each other's expressions clearly. His eyes were enigmatic, she thought, and some demon prompted her to wish to be mysterious herself. Or was it not a wish to be mysterious, she mused, but a genuine sense of bafflement? Or a question mark in her mind as to whether he was serious?

Whatever it was, she suddenly decided, she was

going to leave the lists temporarily, and in a way that might cause *him* some bafflement. If not to say, seriously frustrated...

'Goodnight, Rob,' she murmured. And she slipped her arms around his neck and kissed him in a way that was a serious invitation as well as a sore test of her own willpower.

Then, when he moved convulsively, she freed herself, touched her fingers to his lips, and slipped away across the road.

CHAPTER SEVEN

AT SIX o'clock the next morning, Neve was sitting moodily on a wooden picnic table cemented into the ground beneath the hoop pines across the road from her flat.

She had her bikini on beneath a jumper, and shorts, a shirt and towel in a straw bag beside her. However, if she'd hoped to give Rob Stowe a sleepless night, the plan had rebounded mercilessly on her. Because she'd no sooner got inside after kissing him so—almost wantonly, it occurred to her now—than she'd been consumed by feelings of guilt, *unfair* play and a few other things, yet all things that had made sleep extremely difficult.

But how else to deal with a man who refused to sleep with you before he married you, she asked herself. Who would not—now, out of the blue—entertain the idea of a relationship, a man she was just not sure about?

Of course the dreadful irony of it was that if anyone was puritan by instinct, she was. Which placed her in an invidious position to say the least but...

'Morning, Neve.'

She turned with a start to see him standing behind her, wearing dark green board shorts, a white sloppy joe, with his hair in his eyes, unshaven and still looking half asleep.

'Morning,' she responded, and for the life of her

142

couldn't help the smile that came to her lips. 'Oh, dear. What have I done to you!'

'Dragged me out of bed at an ungodly hour,' he said bitterly. And he hitched himself up to sit on the table beside her, to contemplate the sea darkly.

'Mind you,' he went on, 'I didn't think you looked that chipper yourself.'

'You could only see my back—were you watching me?'

'For about a minute, yes,' he said in a tone that dared her to take issue with this.

'I see. And my back could tell you I was—'

'It was a brooding back, believe me. Could it be that you're not feeling so good about the revenge you took last night, in the light of this yet to be lovely day?'

An unwitting chuckle broke from her lips this time. But she sobered swiftly to see him gazing at her narrowly and not the least amusedly. 'Um...well, it wasn't a very nice thing to do, probably. But it was, if nothing else...' She paused and thought for a bit. 'Something I just couldn't help doing.'

'Are you saying I goaded you into it?'

Neve bit her lip and discovered that it might be fine to castigate herself for her misdemeanours, it was another matter to have this man sitting beside her and being critical.

She shrugged. 'Who knows? I'm going for a swim. So should you, it might put you in a better mood.'

She jumped off the table and strode towards the beach. She didn't stop to see if he was following and when she reached the beach she dumped her bag down, pulled her jumper off and ran into the surf.

The sun was up, giving promise of another cloud-free, glorious day but the water was freezing at first. He'll want to kill me now, she thought as she dived under a wave.

But it seemed Rob Stowe had other ideas. Wet hands reached for her from behind and they both came up spluttering in water about waist deep.

'Let me go,' she gasped.

'No.' He turned her to face him with surprising strength, stared down for one long moment at her body in its violet bikini that matched her eyes, then bent his head and kissed her urgently. But not only that, he slipped his hand beneath her bikini pants and cupped her hips. And he kept kissing her as wave after wave broke around them until she was breathless and helpless and begged him to stop.

He did. And said, 'Good morning, Neve.'

'That was...far more revenge than I took,' she spluttered.

'Was it?' he asked with a smile at the back of his eyes and his hands moving on her slippery body. 'How about I tell you that you look wonderful and you feel absolutely marvellous?'

'I'm sure I look like a drowned rat!'

'No.' He drew her into his arms. 'Like a beautiful siren, quite capable of leading men to shipwreck themselves on the rocks. Last night wasn't that far off it for me.'

She quietened in his arms and laid her cheek against his chest. 'Nor me. I felt dreadful.'

'Let me make a suggestion, then. Should we finish this swim, go and have a good breakfast and see how things look after that?'

Neve raised her head. 'I think that's exactly what we should do.'

He kissed her lightly and let her go, and side by side they dived into the surf again.

He was a powerful swimmer she soon saw and they swam for about an hour, to come out of the water glowing and invigorated.

'You swim really well,' she commented as they towelled themselves down briskly.

'I'm a much better swimmer than I ever was before the accident.'

'Ah! Of course.' She pulled her shirt out of her bag as well as her brush, sunglasses and a hat, and prepared to put the shirt on but he said, 'Why don't we dry off more as we walk up the beach?'

She followed the line of his dark gaze as it slid from the hollows at the base of her throat, to her breasts beneath the violet Lycra, then her waist, her hips—she was flooded with the memory of his hands on them beneath her bikini—and her legs, and she opened her mouth to say something but he intervened.

'It hasn't been my pleasure to walk along a beach somewhere with a gorgeous girl in a bikini for—two years now.'

Neve closed her mouth and studied him candidly in return. His skin was pale but with a definite olive tint and there was a matt of dark hair on his chest, but other than that pale skin on a man with a complexion that would tan readily, there was no other sign that he'd been an invalid. His muscles were sleek and toned, his legs long and strong and his diaphragm taut.

She took a sudden deep breath and looked up at the sky then out to sea and gave herself up to the pure pleasure of being with him. Of being happy with herself in her bikini, conscious of his admiration for her body and very much aware of him in a way that made her skin tingle.

'Neve?'

She looked up at him to see a question in his eyes. 'What are you thinking?'

'All sorts of things,' she replied mysteriously. 'What a lovely day it is. How nice the scenery is—'

'Neve, you're laughing at me!'

She relented. 'Not really. I was thinking that you don't look too bad yourself, Mr. Stowe,' she murmured.

He did absolutely nothing but allow his dark gaze to roam over her again, and perhaps it had something to do with how little she was wearing but it was almost as if he was running his hands down her naked body and she was conscious of the urge to do the same to him, as her nipples peaked beneath the violet Lycra and a rush of sensuous delight came to her.

So much so, she was quite unconscious of anything but Rob Stowe. The other early morning swimmers, joggers and walkers might not have existed as they stood, separated by a foot of white sand but oblivious to anything but the physical effect they had on each other.

And when at last he drew his gaze from the long smooth golden length of her legs to her eyes, they found themselves smiling at each other ruefully.

'Byron Bay obviously does affect people,' she said wryly. 'I feel as if I'm on another planet.'

'So do I but, much as I love Byron,' he drawled, 'I think you have to take the credit for it.'

She looked around then, with a faint smile of disbelief, and she brushed her hair out, stuck her glasses and peaked cap on, and put everything else back into her straw bag. 'Let's go.'

He took her hand and that's how they went along the beach to breakfast, hand in hand.

'Mmm...' Neve patted her stomach about an hour later. 'That was probably quite decadent but lovely.'

She'd had grapefruit to start with, garnished with cherries and mint, then bacon and eggs with fried tomato and banana, and coffee was on its way. The restaurant had a wooden terrace right above the beach and there were birds singing and hopping in the foliage around it. To the east, Cape Byron rose grandly with its sentinel lighthouse.

'We'll have to do some more exercise to get rid of these calories,' he said.

'Are you up to a walk up to the lighthouse this afternoon? It's wonderful up there,' she said enthusiastically and told him about the whale she'd seen.

'Regretfully, not today, Neve.'

She stared at him anxiously. 'Are you all right? Have I—'

'You've done nothing I didn't want to do, and I'm fine. We could always drive up to the lighthouse, though.'

She sat back. 'Of course. So what will we do with our time in between?'

'Unfortunately I have to spend a few hours on the phone and fax. But what say I pick you up around five, we drive up and watch the sun set then I take you to dinner?'

She started to say something then thought better

of it. 'That sounds lovely. Where will we go to dinner?'

'The restaurant at the hotel is very good.'

It occurred to Neve that they were having this conversation in a rather stilted manner. Or, she amended
to herself, that he was lying back in his chair with
his dark eyes curiously watchful of her every reaction. Then she realized that he also looked tired and
her heart started to beat heavily with concern.

'Where's your car, Rob?'

'Why?'

'I thought I could run back and get it and—come
and pick you up. Would you...mind if I did that?'

He smiled briefly. 'That's very kind of you but I
can make it back to the hotel.'

'You should have told me.' She put a hand to her
mouth.

'There was nothing to tell. Other—' he shrugged
'—than that it's going to take a few more months
until I'm fighting fit.'

'Now I feel really dreadful,' she said hollowly.

He raised a wry eyebrow at her.

'For giving you a sleepless night on top of all—
else.'

He laughed softly. 'I think I might have done that
anyway, all off my own bat. OK. Shall we start the
trek home?'

It wasn't far from her flat to his hotel but Neve insisted on accompanying him all the way. 'If you
conked out or something, I'd never forgive myself.'

'Look, I'm sorry about this,' he said as they stood
on the pavement.

'Don't be.' Her eyes danced suddenly. 'You

weren't the only one to have a sleepless night. And—
I also need a bit of time.'

'For what?'

'Oh, this and that,' she said airily.

He looked down at her and the lines beside his
mouth eased a bit. Then he kissed the tip of her nose.
'OK. See you around five.' He walked away stiffly.

Neve watched him until he disappeared. Then
something prompted her to cross the road towards
the beach and find a picnic table to sit down at, and
think deeply. But all that presented itself at first were
the myriad of conflicting emotions within her.

One moment she felt like a young girl in love for
the first time, she mused. A girl who wanted to go
out and buy a new dress because she hadn't brought
anything dressy with her and the restaurant at his
hotel was one of the best in town. A girl who wanted
time to do her hair and nails and savour every delicious moment of anticipation.

A girl, she thought dryly, who had acted purely on
impulse last night, and had surprised the life out of
herself.

But at the same time, she reflected, her more mature, twenty-six-year-old self was still deeply puzzled
by Rob's *marry me or nothing* proposal. Then there
was the side of her that hurt to think of him hurting—
and embedded through it all, the feeling that there
was more to Rob Stowe than she knew, and might
ever know.

She sighed, buried her chin in her hands and stared
out to sea. Then she shook her head, jumped up and
went to buy a dress.

She slipped into a different Range Rover, a hired
one, parked outside her flat at exactly five o'clock.

And neither of them spoke for a long moment.

Until she suddenly said nervously, 'Too much?'

'Not at all. Perfect,' he murmured.

She relaxed. The dress was the colour of old rose gold and very simple. A silk georgette bias-cut slip over a figure-hugging tunic with slender shoulder straps. She wore high gold sandals and a silk, rose-pink rose in her hair where it was swept back on one side, the other side falling loose and shining.

Her nails and lips were painted a matching bronzy pink and just the slightest hint of her favourite per-fume lingered on the air.

She smiled at him as he made not the slightest effort to drive off. 'May I compliment you on your appearance, as well, Mr. Stowe?'

His dark gaze lingered on the smooth, lightly tanned skin of her bare neck and shoulders then he drew his gaze from her at last and looked down at himself ruefully. He had pressed khaki trousers on, a white linen, long-sleeved shirt, his dark hair was damp and tamed and he was freshly-shaved, she guessed.

He said, 'Thank you.'

'Is something wrong, Rob?'

He turned the key on. 'Well—you had me lost for words.' He drove off. 'Did you have that knockout dress in your bag for any special reason?'

'I...' She paused. 'I would love to be able to tell you that I'm always prepared for anything but sadly, it isn't so.'

'You...bought it, today?' he hazarded.

'I did indeed,' she agreed with a quiver of deep

satisfaction in her voice. 'There are some lovely shops in Byron Bay.'

'You didn't have to do that,' he said softly.

'Believe me, Rob, when the urge is upon you to dress up, it's irresistible. If you're a woman.'

He said nothing for a couple of miles, then, 'Oh, hell, Neve, this is extraordinarily difficult.'

'What is?' She heard the sudden wariness in her voice.

'I have to fly back to Sydney tonight. At eight o'clock. A crisis has come up with one of our companies. They're about to go broke not to put too fine a point on it,' he said flatly. 'To make matters worse, the managing director has been embezzling funds and now he's been caught out he's threatening suicide, there are a lot of jobs at risk—'

'Rob,' she broke in, 'why didn't you just tell me this when I first got into the car? Or why,' she heard her voice rise and swallowed, 'why didn't you ring me?' she finished more composedly.

'I only knew myself half an hour ago. Neve—'

'How can you fly out of Byron Bay at such short notice?' she protested.

'Coolangatta is only an hour away and—the company jet is coming to pick me up.'

'Ah. The company jet,' she marvelled. 'What it must be to be so rich.' She laid her head back and clenched her teeth to stop herself from any further gibes arising from unbelievably bitter, black disappointment. But she couldn't stop herself from adding, 'So why are we doing this? Shouldn't you be gone?'

He pulled the Range Rover up in the lighthouse car park. 'Because we still have time to do this,

Neve,' he said levelly and reached over to an esky she hadn't noticed on the back seat.

And from it he pulled a frosted bottle of champagne and two crystal glasses. 'I got them to whip up a snack for us at the hotel. But should we get out and sample the view first?'

'Why not,' she whispered and opened her door.

She was leaning back against the mudguard of the vehicle, staring towards the sunset over the beautiful curve of Byron Bay and its beaches below them, with the lighthouse standing tall and freshly painted a sparkling white behind them, when he joined her a few minutes later. Staring at the patches of light on the water that turned the sea to pewter and the swell that was lifting but not breaking the surface of the water as it came round the cape.

He put a glass of champagne into her hand and said sombrely, 'I'm most abjectly sorry.'

She looked at her champagne through a mist of tears then took a sip to steady herself. 'Don't be. I probably did go over the top, anyway.'

'No.' He put an arm round her shoulder. 'It should have occurred to me. I just didn't think you worried about your appearance greatly.'

'I don't—greatly.'

'That's not to say you don't look smashing all the time.'

She grimaced. 'Smashing? That's a very boyish term.'

'I still meant it.'

Neve stared down at her pink toenails in her strappy gold sandals. 'Does this kind of thing happen often?'

'No more than if I were a doctor, a fireman or a policeman.'

'Clever,' she murmured.

'You're still angry with me, Neve.'

She bit her lip.

'There's an alternative.' He scanned the view for a long moment. 'You could come with me.'

'Oh, I—'

'Because if you're so angry and so disappointed, I think it might be an idea for us to give *serious* thought now to getting married.'

She looked up at him incredulously but his eyes were sober. She said hesitatingly, 'I...look, one of the things I do feel is a bit of a fool and that's probably made me...that's why I'm angry.'

'Is that—by the way, I'm also bitterly disappointed—the only reason do you think, though?'

She moved restlessly. 'I still can't rush into marrying you, Rob.'

'I may not be able to get back before the end of the week.'

They were both silent. Until Neve said unsteadily, 'I don't react well to ultimatums.'

To her utter surprise, he laughed softly and kissed the top of her head. 'Just testing, Miss Williams. OK. Let's see what the hotel has whipped up.'

There was a small tablecloth which he laid over the bonnet. There were smoked salmon sandwiches, homemade cheese straws and spicy meat balls, delicious little sausage rolls as well as a platter of fruit; pineapple, kiwi fruit, strawberries, big luscious black grapes and a selection of cheese and biscuits to go with it. There were plates and silver cutlery, fine linen napkins. There were even two folding canvas chairs.

'I...' Neve said as she sat and sipped her champagne in between nibbling on the goodies, and a golden light enveloped them as well as a marvellous feeling of space, 'I...this is...I'm sorry I was so ungracious. This is rather special.' She raised her glass to him.

'I'm glad,' he said simply. 'I didn't want us to part in anger. And I'm also glad you're wearing your beautiful new dress and looking so—can I say it again?—smashing.'

She smiled faintly. 'We could well be an advertisement for Byron Bay.' This time she raised her glass to the lighthouse and the round rocky dome of Cape Byron.

'There's only one thing I could think of that would be nicer,' he said quietly.

She raised an eyebrow at him.

'To be in bed with you, Neve.'

'I...don't think we should do that to each other, Rob.'

'Not even think about it?' A glint of wry humour lit his eyes.

'You know what difficulties we get ourselves into...that way.'

'Too well,' he replied softly. 'Sleepless nights, ill-humour, a desire for revenge to name a few.'

'I'm tempted to say it's all your doing but that leaves me in a position—I never thought I'd be in,' she murmured.

The golden light was fading and a violet blue sky was now promising dusky shadows. 'What will you do?' he asked.

'For the rest of my holiday? What I did before you came. Swim, walk, read...all the rest of it. And think.' She looked rueful.

'May I wish your thoughts firmly in the direction of how right we are for each other?' he said, and drained his glass.

They stared at each other. He at the curves of her figure beneath the rose gold dress, her lovely bare legs and gold sandals, the way her hair fell—and found himself wondering if she knew that very few things he'd wanted in his life had eluded him. But that he'd also surprised himself at the lengths he was prepared to go to, to secure her in his bed as his wife.

So that she can no longer hide her innermost thoughts and feelings from me behind those beautiful eyes, he asked himself. Let alone walk away from me with that long, free stride. But how is she going to react when she realizes I'm like that—all or nothing and, heaven help me, quite capable of mounting a campaign as if I were taking over another business...

He didn't know that Neve was suddenly thinking along similar lines as she gazed at him. Was this, she wondered, not so much about whether they should sleep together before they married or not but a simple clash of wills?

As the thought came to her, it produced a curious cross-current of emotion in her. An odd little ripple of excitement to think of testing herself against this man, and a realization of having unlocked a part of Rob Stowe that she hadn't known but had dimly worried about. What lengths would he go to, to get his own way?

None of their separate but similar thoughts

changed one thing, however. Nor did it need to be spoken.

He simply took her glass from her, stood up and helped her to her feet and took her in his arms. 'Sorry,' he murmured barely audibly, 'but I can't go without...doing this to us whatever reactions it produces.' And he buried his face in her hair and ran his hands down her back from her shoulders to her hips.

Neve stood stock-still for a moment, then with a little sigh, she slipped her arms around his neck and offered him her mouth.

It was dark when they drew apart, and it was impossible, she found, to speak. Because her emotions might be in turmoil but her body was singing. All her senses were alive with a response to the feel of him against her. She felt vibrant and alive as never before, it was a joy to feel his hands on her breasts, it was wonderful to run her own hands down his back, to lay her lips on his skin where his shirt opened at the throat, to press herself against him and be crushed in his arms.

And it was cruelly cold and almost unbearable to be parted from him.

They packed up in silence, and he drove her back to her apartment without saying anything, although he did once put his hand over hers as they lay entwined, with her knuckles showing white, in her lap.

Then he pulled up and reached into his trouser pocket. 'You're not the only one who went shopping today.'

She turned to him wide-eyed as he put a small, beautifully wrapped parcel in her lap.

'No, don't open it now,' he added. 'And ring me as soon as you get home. Goodbye, for now.'

He put his long fingers under her chin and kissed her lightly.

Neve hesitated then kissed him back and slipped out of the car.

It was a ring, a square sapphire with two diamonds on either side and it was exquisite. There was also a very brief note.

My dear Neve, she read, with this ring, may we get engaged?

For a long while she simply stared at the ring. Then her hand hovered over it a couple of times but each time she stopped herself from touching it. Finally she put the little box on the table and wandered out onto her balcony to do battle with her strange thoughts.

How could she possibly be committing herself to Rob Stowe just by putting on his ring? He wasn't even there, he couldn't know whether she'd tried it on or not. It was only a ring not any kind of a bond between them unless she wanted it to be. Shouldn't *he* be the one to put it on anyway—shouldn't he be *there* with her now!

And she suddenly saw the nature of her dilemma. Deep within she was still angry at being forced to play second fiddle to his business empire, and no ring, lovely as it was, was going to take away that hurt and anger.

All of which, she told herself, is a recipe for disaster—another one. Not that she visualized herself as a possessive wife but this was a special time for them if they were thinking of spending the rest of their lives together—there had to be some sacred times when business couldn't intrude, surely?

Which brought her other things back to mind, she mused. Such as a clash of wills with a man who liked to get his own way—she couldn't rid her mind of the thought that had crept into it up on Cape Byron where, although they'd been utterly absorbed in one another, she had sensed the shadow of something else between them.

She sighed and turned to go back inside. And as she gazed down at his ring again, Molly Condren came to mind. Who, by her own admission, had not had the particular strength of mind required not to be flattened by Rob Stowe. Was she, Neve Williams, any more capable of resisting it?

Then sheer human nature got the better of her. She plucked the ring from its bed of white velvet and slipped it on. It fitted, it suited the shape of her hand and had she seen it first, she would probably have chosen it herself. But none of that made her any more sure that she should get engaged to Rob Stowe, let alone marry him. She took it off and put it away in its box.

'Neve, you look wonderful!' George Maitland said enthusiastically the next Monday morning.

'Thank you!' She smiled at him.

'Where did you go?'

'Not the Seychelles, George, just Byron Bay.'

'Ah, good old Byron,' George marvelled. 'You can't beat it! Anything interesting happen to you up there?'

Neve started to say, quite untruthfully, that no, nothing had happened to her but she stopped suddenly and looked at her editor more closely. 'What do you mean, George?'

'Your love life, for example? I just happened to propose to my wife on Clarks Beach in the moonlight then we went for a skinny-dip—long time ago now, though, but that's what Byron Bay can do to you.'

Neve relaxed at the same time as she thought, you're not wrong! And an imp of humour made her eyes dance. 'How very daring, George!'

'Well, people do skinny-dip a lot at Byron but it was nearly a disaster—we couldn't find our clothes when we came out—the moon had disappeared behind some clouds.'

Neve burst out laughing. 'Truly?'

'Not for at least forty-five minutes. My wife was getting hysterical. So, you didn't bump into Rob Stowe by any chance?'

Neve stopped laughing abruptly. 'What do you mean?'

'Brent picked up a whisper that he was up there with someone who *wasn't* Molly Condren. And talking of our beloved Molly, have you heard that she's going to star in the new TV series the ABC's making?'

'Yes. Brent isn't...you're not going to let him...?' Neve ran out of words.

'Run with an unsubstantiated bit of gossip? Not at this stage, no, Neve.'

She sat back, unable to suppress the sigh of relief that escaped her.

'No,' George repeated thoughtfully as he eyed her shrewdly. 'But we're not the only paper in town, remember that. Now, I've got this assignment for you—a big one. She could be the next leader of the

Australian Labour Party and she's been interviewed many a time before but I'd like a...woman-to-woman slant, Neve.'

Neve wrested her mind from his previous remarks with difficulty. Had it been a warning that she and Rob were about to be splashed over the pages of another paper? 'Uh...you mean...?'

'None other. Go to it, Neve. She's in Sydney for this week and she's agreed to spend a morning with you.'

'Yes, George,' Neve said feebly.

He smiled down at her, patted her on the back and walked away.

When Neve got home that night, the message light on her answering machine was blinking. Rob, she thought. What was she going to say to him? Her remaining days at Byron had not yielded any bursts of inspiration. But something told her it would be futile to ignore him.

She showered and changed into something cool first. Summer had come to Sydney with a vengeance. Then she picked up the phone.

'Hi,' she said when she got through to him. 'How are you?'

'As lonely as hell and correspondingly cross,' he replied. 'Why don't you come over and have a swim? Or were you planning to ignore me?'

'Strange you should say that. Something told me I shouldn't.'

There was a moment of silence as if he was feeling his way around this. Then he said, 'Put yourself in a taxi, Jude has made dinner for us. See you soon.' And he put the phone down.

Neve took the receiver from her ear and stared at it incredulously. Then she reminded herself that she was carrying his engagement ring in her purse, afraid to let it out of her sight, and—she drew a deep breath—somehow or other she had to find the words to tell him they wouldn't suit.

Judy let her in and told her she looked lovely and summery. 'Rob's waiting for you outside—it's a beaut evening for a swim although dinner isn't that far away,' she added.

As a matter of fact, Rob Stowe was gardening when Neve stepped outside. He had a hose in one hand and a pair of secateurs in the other and he didn't appear to hear her immediately. He wore a pair of old navy boards shorts, no shoes and a faded yellow shirt—and it was the last thing she'd expected to see him doing.

Then he turned and his dark gaze wandered over her cool, apple-green cotton, halter-neck dress and her matching green patent mules. He turned the hose off, dumped the secateurs on a cane lounger and held out his hand.

Neve stirred, and as if in a dream, walked towards him.

'Hi,' he said softly as their hands touched. 'I've missed you.'

'I…me, too,' she said huskily, because she had.

He raised her hand to his mouth and kissed her knuckles then looked at it—it was her left hand, and it was quite bare. But all he did was raise a wry eyebrow at her then he told her to sit down while he got them a drink.

It was almost dark when he came back with two tall glasses and put one in her hand.

'A mint julep,' he murmured. He picked up what looked like a remote control from the table between them, pressed a button, and underwater lights came on in the pool making it look wonderfully inviting.

'That's impressive,' she said. 'I didn't know you liked to garden.'

'It's my hobby,' he replied, sitting down. 'I designed it and did the work—and I can't tell you how nice it is not to have to do it from a wheelchair now.'

She looked around. And realized she'd been sure a landscape gardener had been hired to create this fragrant, leafy little paradise in the middle of Sydney as well as to maintain it, which made her feel suddenly uncomfortable.

'What?' he asked with a wicked little glint in his eyes. 'No, don't tell me. You thought only money had been expended to create my garden?'

'I...yes, I did,' she confessed. 'Sorry.'

'Does that mean I might be more likeable than you'd also thought?' he drawled.

Shock made her gaze jerk to his, then away abruptly and some colour flowed into her cheeks. 'I...have I ever said I didn't like you?' she countered, however.

'No, but something's in the air. You're not wearing the ring, you didn't call me although you've been home since yesterday afternoon—how was the rest of your stay in Byron, by the way?'

'Fine.' She shook her head as if to make the adjustment to a rather startling switch of topics, then she wondered if it was really a switch of topics, or if he knew by some mysterious process that the rest of her stay in Byron Bay had been haunted by memories of him.

'If you're going to have a quick dip,' Judy said, coming out of the conservatory, 'I just thought I'd let you know that dinner will be ready to be served in about a quarter of an hour. I wouldn't hassle you like this,' she added anxiously, 'but I've arranged to go to a movie with my sister.'

'Thanks, Jude—no problem, we'll be ready when you are! Are we going to swim?' he said to Neve when Judy had retired.

'I didn't...I didn't bring my togs. Rob, I don't know how to tell you this but I can't do it.' And she searched her purse for the velvet box, and put it on the table between them.

He looked at it then raised his eyebrows at her but said nothing.

Neve bit her lip. 'Look, Rob, I get the feeling we're just too strong-minded for each other. I have,' she paused then looked at him levelly, 'this premonition that it's all very well to talk of our independence causing us never to be bored with each other but, well, you're a man who likes to get his own way. I may have the same problem.'

'What if,' he said slowly, 'what we want happens to be the same thing?'

She frowned and grasped one implication of his question. 'You don't mind admitting you like to get your own way?'

'No. Nor do you by the sound of it. This could be bigger than our individual wills, though.'

Something made her smile faintly.

'Tell me?' he murmured.

'It's nothing.'

'So what do you suggest we do?'

His question hung in the air.

Neve sipped her mint julep. 'I don't know. Please don't think I didn't like the ring, it's beautiful. But—' She shrugged.

'May I see it on?'

'No, Rob.' Tension claimed her suddenly and she put her glass down with a little clatter and stood up.

He didn't move. 'Are you about to run away, Neve?'

Something in the tone of his voice caused her hackles to rise.

'What's the point of staying?'

'Jude has made us a special dinner—if for no other reason,' he said dryly.

Neve breathed exasperatedly.

'Perhaps we could discuss how to stay—just friends?'

'You know very well how impossible that would be.' Neve stopped abruptly.

'Precisely,' he said quite coolly.

And the long-suffering Judy reappeared to tell them that dinner was served, sealing Neve's fate.

There was a prawn cocktail to start with. And tall yellow candles on the table casting a gentle glow over them.

'Where's Oliver?' Neve asked, as she sat down.

'In Townsville with Portia. He's a seasoned traveller.'

Neve picked up her fork. 'Have you found them a house?'

'Yes, I have. A couple of blocks away in this

street. It needs a bit of renovation and redecorating but Molly's good at that.'

'So when does Portia come home to you?'

'In a couple of weeks.' He finished his cocktail and laid down his fork. 'I never got around to showing you her work.'

Neve patted her mouth with a napkin and smiled up at Judy as she appeared to take their plates. 'That was delicious. Thank you. I would love to know how you made that sauce.'

Judy's face lit up. 'I'll write it out for you!'

She bustled out and reappeared with a steaming casserole, a dish of rice and a dish of vegetables.

'Thanks, Jude,' Rob said as he opened a bottle of wine. 'Why don't you hop off now?'

'Oh, but there's dessert and—'

'We can help ourselves and I promise not to leave a big mess for you tomorrow. I'm sure Neve and I can handle a few dishes.' He raised an eyebrow at Neve.

'Of...of course we can.'

'Well, if you're sure you don't mind, it is—' Judy consulted her watch '—getting just a little bit late.'

'Off you go,' Rob said affectionately. 'Enjoy the movie and say hi to your sister for me.'

Judy beamed at him then at Neve, and left.

'So,' he remarked as he poured the wine then sat down again, 'we're on our own.'

'As you so carefully engineered,' she said with a little glint of anger in her eyes.

He looked at her quizzically. 'You begrudge Jude time to go to the movies without having to rush around madly?'

'You know very well I don't! It has nothing to do with it!' she protested.

'Then what is your problem, Neve?' He looked at her coolly.

'Your machinations. The way you plot and plan things. The way,' she said deliberately, 'you've ensured that I don't leave here at least until I've done the dishes because you know damn well I wouldn't do that to Judy!'

'Oh, that,' he said casually although the way he was watching her was anything but casual. 'Now you mention it, it doesn't seem any worse to me to do a bit of sensible planning rather than the haphazard way you go about things.'

'Hap...what are you *talking* about?'

'Well, you kiss me with extreme passion yet you won't marry me. You refuse to be friends with me because *you* know damn well we can't keep our hands off each other, and now,' he said with soft, deadly satire, 'you don't even want to talk about it. Which leads me to wonder what you would call it, Neve?'

CHAPTER EIGHT

NEVE controlled her anger by a sheer effort of will.

He waited for a moment then lifted the lid of the casserole and the delicious aroma of beef in burgundy assailed their nostrils. 'Ah. One of my favourites,' he murmured. 'I hope beef doesn't affect you as oysters and calamari do?'

'Not normally,' Neve replied sweetly. 'Tonight it would stick in my throat, however.'

'You know, if you married me, you wouldn't have any of these problems. Does any of this go back to me having to leave you so suddenly in Byron Bay?' he queried, and began to dish up the beef and rice, two plates, she noticed.

'Yes, as a matter of fact it does.' She stared at the plate he put in front of her. 'And not because I made a fool of myself—'

'I told you that wasn't the case.'

'Thank you,' she said with irony. 'But what got to me was the feeling that although I might be an unfinished bit of business, I certainly wasn't the most important bit of business—that night was special, Rob. I felt special, I tried to look special and I was on the verge of putting a lid on all my doubts and taking the plunge.'

Neither of them had started to eat as he stared at her steadily. Then he said, 'So tell me more about your doubts.'

She picked up her wineglass and studied the red

depths. Then her shoulders slumped suddenly. 'I'm afraid of you, I guess. Afraid that I'll be no better than Molly at—surviving you.'

'Do you really think I'd want to marry you, Neve, if I had any fears on that score?' he asked quietly.

'But you may not know me—as I know me,' she whispered. 'And you are pressuring me.' She gestured wearily.

'All right. Let's take another tack. Let's see how we go without each other for a while. Eat your dinner,' he added gently.

She started to eat automatically. Then she said, 'How long did you have in mind?'

'As long as you like.'

Her eyes widened. 'No...contact at all?'

'If that's what you want.'

'That wouldn't help me to get to know you any better,' she said with a helpless kind of confusion.

'Then—' he lay back and looked at her with amusement '—we may have to surround ourselves with people.'

'Rob, this isn't funny!'

'No,' he agreed. 'Well, actually I think it does have a funny side to it but I'm sure I won't be laughing for long.' And his gaze swept over her in a way that left her in no doubt as to his meaning.

She trembled suddenly and she saw his eyes register it although he didn't comment. Then she was surprised to find she'd finished her beef and she picked up her wineglass again. But in the end she put it down untasted and start to laugh.

He raised his eyebrows at her.

'I'm just wondering whether I'm mad—most women would give their eye teeth to be in this position with you, I'm sure. But—I think it would be a good idea if we did have a little break.'

'Surrounded by others or not?'

'I don't know where or how we could do that—'

'I've been invited to dinner on Friday night. Would you care to come with me?'

'In aid of anything particular?' she asked.

'It's Bunny's fiftieth birthday.' He named an exclusive restaurant. 'Toni will be there, naturally.'

'What about—Molly?'

'No, she's staying in Townsville for another week.'

Neve grimaced. 'That's…sort of…making it rather public, isn't it?'

'Not really. I promise not to canoodle with you during the event. And you do know the Fanshawes, as well as Toni.'

'Canoodle?' Her eyes danced for a moment.

'Kiss, cuddle, appear to be absolutely obsessed with you,' he said gravely. 'That kind of thing.'

'All right,' Neve said slowly.

'I'm sure it would be a fitting event to wear your beautiful new dress to.'

Neve smiled faintly and said, 'It was beautiful up there—oh, hell. I honestly don't know what to do!'

'Let's just give it a rest for a while,' he murmured. 'And feast ourselves on Jude's dessert.'

He was as good as his word for the rest of the evening.

They ate homemade apple pie with cream then she insisted on clearing up and he insisted on helping, but he kept it all light and easy. She made coffee and they drank it outside, talking about nothing very much although she told him about her next assignment.

'Ah. Now she might be even harder to interview than I was,' he drawled.

'You know her?'

'Yes, very well, as a matter of fact.' He grinned suddenly.

'So what could be so difficult about her?'

'Getting a word in edgeways. She's a powerful talker and she's an extremely hard person to say no to. All the same, give her my best regards.'

'I...all right.'

He stretched suddenly and yawned then looked surprised.

Neve got up. 'Must be all that gardening,' she said, and kissed him lightly on the forehead. 'No, don't get up. I can let myself out. And thank you for—understanding. I'll see you on Friday night.'

She walked away and was not to see how Rob Stowe suddenly clenched his hands around the arms of his chair. Nor was she to know that he cursed himself fluently for persistently pressing all the wrong keys. What was it that was stopping him from simply telling her there was no way he could live without her? The fear of failure, he thought suddenly.

'Have I met you before somewhere?' Lucy Cameron, politician and who, some believed, could be the next leader of the Labour Party, said to Neve with a frown.

They were in her hotel suite and had just met.

'I don't think so, Mrs. Cameron. I'm sure I would have remembered.'

'I've the feeling I've seen your face somewhere,

that's all.' Lucy Cameron was in her fifties, and she was a tall, striking woman but renowned for her warmth and her 'common touch.'

'I believe we do have an acquaintance in common, though,' Neve murmured and immediately wondered why she'd said it. She'd had no intention of mentioning Rob. 'Uh—Rob Stowe asked me to pass on his regards.'

Lucy clapped her forehead. 'That's it! So you're the mystery woman in Rob's life!'

'Oh, n—'

But Lucy was up and rifling frantically through a paper. 'There,' she said triumphantly and handed Neve a page.

There could be no mistaking either of them in the picture, captured as they were walking hand in hand along a beach, and smiling into each other's eyes. And the caption said: *Millionaire businessman Rob Stowe appears to have come out of seclusion at last after a near-fatal accident two years ago. Captured here at beautiful Byron Bay with a mystery lady although not that long ago he was seen squiring Molly Condren about.*

Neve dropped the paper and put a hand to her mouth. And she said foolishly, 'George did warn me but I—forgot.'

'Well, I want to hear all about it,' Lucy insisted. 'I've known Rob for years, you see.'

And that's how the tables were turned on Neve who had come to interview Lucy Cameron, only to find herself being given the third degree and unable to resist although that may also have had something to do with sheer shock...

'I'll give you a little tip,' Lucy said after she'd

wrested a lot more from Neve than she would have dreamt she could have told anyone. 'You have to handle men, you see. It's no good expecting them to understand us, poor things, without a good bit of help along the way.'

A smile trembled on Neve's lips.

'However, Rob is a particularly determined man and the thought of failure doesn't come easily to him—he would never have got where he is today otherwise, and he might just never have walked again for that matter.'

'I...I know,' Neve said slowly.

'Then try laying down your arms, my dear. I'm pretty certain that once he doesn't feel threatened by failure—and he knows *exactly* what its like to stare that in the face after his accident—you might see a much more reasonable man.'

Neve stared at her with widening eyes. 'Oh,' she said. 'I never thought of that but—he won't let me until we're married.'

'Neve,' Lucy reproved, 'surely a beautiful girl like yourself must have some...way of overcoming that.'

Neve gazed at Lucy Cameron and a tinge of pink came to her cheeks.

Lucy patted her hand. 'I see we understand each other. The other thing is, much as I love her, Molly would have sent him crazy. Well, what would you like to know about me?'

'Where do you get your wisdom regarding men from?' Neve asked with suddenly dancing eyes.

But of course what might have sounded sane and rational at the time, despite coming as an absolute surprise, was a different matter when she thought about it on her own.

What if he wasn't haunted by the spectre of failure, if it wasn't the reason for the pressure he'd applied? Then again, *he* had suggested this break. Was he feeling as lonely and miserable?

Damn, she said to herself, what does one do if you think you may not be able to live with a man but living without him is a version of hell?

Then there was George she had to deal with.

'Told you,' he said when she got to work the next morning. 'Although may I say you might have told me!'

'There's nothing to tell. It…we…look, George, no comment,' she said frustratedly.

George looked amused. He also said with a fatherly air, 'Neve, I suspected this was in the air from the day you sat there with a sprained ankle and didn't want to go back to interview him. Can I give you a bit of advice—I will anyway,' he continued when she moved restlessly.

'No, just listen,' he said, 'When two planets collide there's a lot of fireworks. Don't forget you can be a cool, tough customer. But you've got to make the guy some allowances. He's come back on a long, hard road—he may not be quite as rational as you are about some things.'

Once again Neve stared at someone with widening eyes. 'How do you…I mean,' she stammered and couldn't go on.

'Know that you two are giving each other a tough time? I'd say it was almost inevitable, knowing you both. But just go a little easy on him, you could be surprised.'

She didn't believe she was hearing this—if anyone was the unconfident one, wasn't it her? But it stayed with her and wouldn't let her go. All through that uncomfortable week of fielding comments from her colleagues and other journalists as word seeped out. But she stuck to a simple but firm *no comment,* and she didn't hear a thing from Rob until he came to pick her up on Friday night.

'Well, well,' he murmured as he came though her doorway, 'does this give you a feeling of déjà vu, Neve?'

His dark gaze drifted over her lovely rose gold dress, the same sandals, the same flower in her hair.

'Yes.' She studied him in return in his dark suit and had difficulty in suppressing the tremor that ran through her. 'Although I can't help wishing I was at Cape Byron with you—not that Byron Bay turned out to be a very private spot.'

'You saw the picture in the paper?' He shrugged when she nodded. 'That's the price of fame, sometimes.'

'So it didn't upset you?'

'No. How about you?'

'I…well, I was just worried about Molly and Portia and what they would think.'

'Molly rang me. She said she didn't know why it hadn't occurred to her before but she thought you might be perfect for me.'

Neve stared up into his eyes. 'Are you serious? I mean, was she serious?'

He took her hand. 'Yes. And Portia thinks it couldn't have worked out better. I had a long chat with her. She said Molly was like a new person. She said, *"You have to understand Mum. She really thought she was doing what would be best for me by giving me my father and mother but now she knows how blind she was being."'*

'That—' Neve closed her eyes briefly '—is such a weight off my mind.'

He kissed her knuckles then let go of her hand. 'Sorry, that wasn't supposed to be on the agenda but—'

'No, come in,' she invited.

He glanced at his watch. 'We don't have much time.'

She didn't answer but led the way into her living room. There was a bottle of champagne on ice and a tray of snacks on her dining table but only two glasses. The overhead lights were off but there were two lamps on and a gold candle in a candle glass, and the lilt of Vivaldi coming from her CD player

He frowned and looked at her with a raised eyebrow.

'We're not going to the party, Rob,' she said quietly.

'But—isn't it a little late to cancel out?'

'I did that this morning. Bunny quite understands—and there are fifty other people going.'

'So...?'

She moistened her lips. 'You told me that getting married before I slept with you was the way I would rather do things. It's not—but not because I don't want to marry you. It's also what I'd like to do now, tonight.'

'Why?' But he reached for her hand again.

'Because I love you, Rob. There may be all sorts

of difficulties but nothing can change that,' she said simply. 'And even although I was still unsure about Molly and Portia, they couldn't change it, either.'

'Neve…' He said her name on a breath but there was still a frown in his eyes.

'You see,' she said, 'it suddenly came to me that to be afraid of failure before you even give something a chance, is faint-hearted. Are you ever afraid of failure, Rob?'

He put his hands on her shoulders. 'How did you *know?*' he said intensely. 'I…watched you walk away from me on Monday night, and it all came home to me, that it was a desperate fear of failure that was stopping me from saying—I can't live without you, Neve. I'm…I love you more than I thought was possible yet I didn't even see that was why I left you in Byron, a fear of failure. But—' He stopped abruptly.

'Go on,' she whispered.

'How do you know it's the same for you?'

'Because I've been living without you for months now, Rob. And it's been lonelier than I'd thought possible. It's been like a continual ache and is if I was hollow, somehow.'

He closed his eyes and took her into his arms. 'I kept thinking, deep down, that I'd beaten the odds quite a bit in my life, especially lately, and was my luck about to run out? Over the one thing that mattered more to me than all the others. Neve, I…I can be blind and stupid but I did honestly think you would be happier to wait.'

'Shush. I know all the things you can be.' She looked into his eyes. 'I can be a few things, too. And thank you for wanting to do things the way you thought I might want to do them. The thing is, I can't wait—I'm...all waited out.'

But his eyes were suddenly sombre. 'I have to tell you that the other reason *I* wanted to wait was—all tied up with my male ego. I thought, at least if she's married to me, if I am no bloody good in bed, we'll be able to...work on it.'

'Oh, Rob,' she said on a breath, but he wouldn't let her go on.

'Unfortunately, when you've been through...' He paused then said with a sigh, 'Things like a complete lack of control of your functions, when your nervous system just doesn't respond to signals from your brain, when—well, you know all the gory details—you can't help a slight lack of confidence. Although, when you're in my arms like this—'

'Should we just concentrate on that?' she broke in gently. 'You know, Rob, we're two of a kind in this. Had you forgotten that I might need help, too?'

He held her so tight that for a moment she couldn't breathe.

Much later he brought them each a glass of champagne.

There was a bedside lamp on and it cast a soft glow over Neve, lying beneath a blue and sea green sheet with her hair spread out on the pillow.

He looked down at her for a long moment before he put both glasses down and sat on the side of the bed. She turned over and taking the sheet with her moved to rest on her elbows beside him. He slid a hand through her hair and she moved again, this time to curl her legs up and sit up across his lap resting on her hands. He spread his fingers across her back and she lifted her face to his and closed her eyes.

Their mouths touched, just touched but it was electric and in that static moment, there seemed to flow between all that was devastatingly sensual, all the joy, the wonder and rapturous intimacy of their union. He kissed her then cast the sheet aside and ran his hand down the curve of her hips and up to stroke her breasts. 'You're so beautiful,' he said huskily.

'Rob,' she breathed against his mouth, 'there seems to be a new dimension to me, I feel so different.'

'Tell me,' he invited.

'I don't think I really believed joy and sheer rapture like that, actually existed.'

'Not even when you insisted on sleeping with me?' He lifted his head and his dark eyes were suddenly wicked.

'Put it this way, the scale of it was more than I'd expected in my wildest dreams.'

He said nothing for a long moment. Then, 'You're right. It was like nothing else I've known.'

'I love it when you do that.'

He plucked her nipple and she arched her back. She heard him take a deep, unsteady breath and his hands were momentarily hard on her body as he moved her so he could lie beside her. Then he was caressing her with his fingertips and she felt the sensations of desire flow through her, and the loveliness of being ready to receive him again, the satisfaction of knowing that he was experiencing as much as she was.

'Now?' he said into her hair.

'Yes, please, now or I might die.'

He took her and once again brought her the joy and rapture she hadn't known could exist on such a scale, and he himself shuddered in the grip of their climax.

And when it finally subsided and they were able to speak again, they pushed their pillows up against the bed head so they could sit up and lean back and, holding hands, sipped their champagne.

'I thought once before that you made my body sing,' she said. 'Now I know it was only a faint chorus to what you can do when you really set your mind to it.'

'You say the nicest things,' he murmured then looked at her with wicked little glints in his eyes again. 'However, I have to tell you that *I* feel…like the cat who's got the cream.'

'Don't think you're alone in that, Mr. Stowe,' she said gravely.

'Very much satisfied?' he queried with a faint little smile.

'Oh, more than that,' Neve replied grandly. 'Positively smug!'

He laughed and kissed her. 'I was hesitating to say that myself but the truth is I feel like a new man and a *very* smug one. I also, I have to warn you, Miss Williams, am now, well, I didn't think it was possible to be more in love with you but I am.' His hand tightened on hers.

'I know—'

'You do?' He glinted a laughing little look at her although there was something else in his eyes, as well.

'I was going to say—' she looked injured '—that I know the feeling. What are we going to do?'

'This minute or…?'

'I mean,' she said a little helplessly, 'I've got the feeling it's going to be really difficult to hide from everyone that I'm no longer such a cool, tough character.' She grimaced.

'Will you feel you need to hide it?' he asked. 'I don't intend to hide this new me from anyone.'

'You may not show it as much as I do,' she said humorously.

'And you may have trouble getting me out of this bed let alone this flat,' he responded.

'No—after-effects?' She looked at him with sudden anxiety.

He touched her cheek. 'None. Just a wonderful feeling of peace.'

She relaxed. 'It is the weekend. I don't have to go anywhere.'

He removed her empty glass from her hand and pulled her close to him. 'Neither do I, Neve. Just think of that. Never again do I have to do battle with the cold, empty spaces that don't hold you.'

'You're not too bad with words yourself,' she whispered.

In the event, they did go out, but not until Sunday afternoon.

They went to see Toni, who took one look at them standing on her doorstep and said, 'I knew it! You two were made for each other. When's the wedding?'

'This wedding,' Rob said that evening.

They were in his house sitting with their arms

around each other on the fuschia settee.

Neve kissed his throat. 'My mother will be very pleased with you, Rob Stowe. Do you mind a white wedding with all the trimmings?'

He stroked her hair. 'No. Why should I?'

'But would you mind—I've drifted away from my family a bit since I came down here—could we have it up there? Then they'd know I do love them even although I got a bit carried away about being a career girl—you made me see that,' she added with a tinge of wonder in her voice.

'Neve,' he tilted her chin then kissed her lips. 'Taking the last point first, I would never stop you from being a journalist.'

'Thanks,' she said huskily, 'and I've thought about it. I don't honestly think I *could* ever stop myself from writing but now I've established a bit of a reputation, and now I'm about to be a married lady—' her lips curved '—I think freelancing is the way to go. A lot of journalism is done on that basis anyway and I wouldn't be tied down to a nine-to-five job—'

'You don't have to—'

'Yes I do. And gladly. I look upon it as a challenge and I'm sure George—well, he's given me enough advice to—that is to say...' She trailed off.

'What has George given you advice about?' he asked ruefully.

'This and that,' Neve said airily. 'It turned out to be very good advice it so happens—'

'Not to do with you and I?'

'I think I'll preserve a mysterious silence on the subject.'

But Rob laid his head back and laughed. 'My old mate, George!'

'Not only your old mate George,' she said wryly. 'Your old mate Lucy Cameron.'

'Have I been handled?' he asked ominously, but his eyes were still laughing.

'I think we've both been handled all the way through—yes. Do you mind?' she asked, suddenly serious. 'Because I can only thank heavens someone was able to get it through my dense head what I was about to walk away from.'

He didn't tell her what he thought but showed her. They drew apart and it took some time for their breathing to steady.

'I love you,' he said. 'It started out with your eyes and the way you walk, how cool and clever you were, but now it's the way you laugh, the way you sleep, it's like watching a flower open and finding joy, warmth and so much more.' He touched her face with his fingertips. 'You told me that you hadn't believed the scale of certain things that could happen between a man and a woman. I have to tell you I've only seen the surface of a woman before.'

'Rob,' she said barely audibly.

'Let me finish. Of course there were times when it was good but never like this. Never to have and hold an enchanted creature and not know what words to say to her.'

'Yes you have...'

'Not really. You've done most of the talking.'

She bit her lip and he smiled faintly and brushed it with his thumb.

'But that's because in my heart I've been struck dumb because you had the faith and the courage to see through the ridiculous defences I was building and cut through them,' he said softly.

'I did have some help.'

'All the help in the world wouldn't have made it any easier. Do you think I don't know that, Neve?'

They gazed at each other. 'Right up until the last minute I wasn't sure,' she confessed. 'But then, suddenly, it didn't seem to matter whether I'd got it right or wrong. I just knew I needed you. I...couldn't be whole without you.

'I wonder if you have any idea how much I need you and always will?'

'Thank heavens,' she said fervently and clung to him.

'This wedding...'

This time Neve said it. She went on, 'There is a lovely old wooden church in the town nearest to the station—it's where I was christened and confirmed. And there's a church hall—Rob—' she sat up anxiously '—it's a long, long way from Woollahra.'

'That's perfectly fine with me.'

'But your family, your friends—'

'Would there be any motels or hotels in the town?'

'Yes, four but—'

'Then we have accommodation, what else is there to worry about? By the way, have I told you I love you lately?'

She subsided with a grin. 'So you really don't mind?'

He kissed her. 'I think it's very right that you should be married in the church where you were confirmed and christened, and where your family can be at home on such a wonderful day and be in command to be able to do it as they would like to.'

A month later there was not a room to be had in one outback Western Queensland town and the church was packed to capacity as Neve started to walk down the aisle on the arm of her father.

A murmur ran through the throng because she'd never looked more lovely or radiant and did they but know it, secretly astounded out how well this blending of some of the cream of Sydney society and the country people she'd known all her life and grown up with, was going.

She did know that she had to thank Rob for it, though. From the moment he'd met her parents and her brothers, he'd somehow contrived to let them know what he felt for her, he'd been respectful with her father, had charmed her mother and been accepted by her brothers, no mean feat, she thought wryly.

And there was no doubting that they were all extremely happy for her and bursting with pride, her mother especially. And thanks to her, there was a marvellous feast laid out in the church hall.

There were also some extremely elegant women in the congregation, Rob's own mother in the palest green, Molly Condren looking divine in delphinium blue with a cartwheel hat that would be talked about for years, Antonia Simpson in caramel Thai silk. Even Bunny Fanshawe, for once in her life, was coordinated in a simple, stylish garnet suit.

And then there was Portia, walking in front of Neve in her first long dress and radiating both excitement and happiness.

Neve looked down at her own dress as she drew abreast of the family pew, then looked into her mother's eyes and saw sheer happiness. Because throughout all her years of maternity and domesticity and her sometime dissatisfaction with her life, Mary Williams had preserved her slim white satin wedding dress and clouds of veil perfectly, and Neve wore them today.

Thank you, Neve mouthed silently to her mother as she passed, and could only thank God herself, that she had passed out of that zone where she'd distanced herself from her mother, especially, and now could love and understand her.

Then she was standing beside the tall, silent man who was to become her husband and one glance at him told her he was rather pale and she could sense how tense he was.

And as her father put her hand on Rob's arm, she thought she knew why and it brought sudden tears to her eyes. But it was only when the bulk of the service was over and the minister told Rob Stowe that he may kiss the bride, that she was able to put it into words.

He lifted her veil and stared into her violet eyes.

'Don't ever doubt me again, Rob,' she whispered with tears again but laughter in her eyes.

'How did you know?'

'I just knew. But now I'm not only yours, I'm officially and legally yours.'

He took her in his arms and you could have heard a pin drop. 'Neve,' he said, quite audibly to the whole church, 'I was desperately afraid you'd change your mind at the last minute because, as I told you once but now I'd like to tell the whole world, I just couldn't live without you, my darling.'

The congregation erupted into a cheer of delight that threatened to raise the roof, and he started to kiss her.

George Maitland also said proudly to his wife, 'You know, *I* started all this.'

London's streets aren't just paved with gold—they're home to three of the world's most eligible bachelors!

You can meet these gorgeous men, and the women who steal their hearts, in:

NOTTING HILL GROOMS

Look out for these tantalizing romances set in London's exclusive Notting Hill, written by highly acclaimed authors who, between them, have sold more than 35 million books worldwide!

Irresistible Temptation by Sara Craven
Harlequin Presents® #2077
On sale December 1999

Reform of the Playboy by Mary Lyons
Harlequin Presents® #2083
On sale January 2000

The Millionaire Affair by Sophie Weston
Harlequin Presents® #2089
On sale February 2000

Available wherever Harlequin books are sold.

HARLEQUIN®
Makes any time special ™

Visit us at www.romance.net

HPNHG

If you enjoyed what you just read,
then we've got an offer you can't resist!

Take 2 bestselling
love stories FREE!
Plus get a FREE surprise gift!

Clip this page and mail it to Harlequin Reader Service®

IN U.S.A.	IN CANADA
3010 Walden Ave.	P.O. Box 609
P.O. Box 1867	Fort Erie, Ontario
Buffalo, N.Y. 14240-1867	L2A 5X3

YES! Please send me 2 free Harlequin Presents® novels and my free surprise gift. Then send me 6 brand-new novels every month, which I will receive months before they're available in stores. In the U.S.A., bill me at the bargain price of $3.12 plus 25¢ delivery per book and applicable sales tax, if any*. In Canada, bill me at the bargain price of $3.49 plus 25¢ delivery per book and applicable taxes**. That's the complete price and a savings of over 10% off the cover prices—what a great deal! I understand that accepting the 2 free books and gift places me under no obligation ever to buy any books. I can always return a shipment and cancel at any time. Even if I never buy another book from Harlequin, the 2 free books and gift are mine to keep forever. So why not take us up on our invitation. You'll be glad you did!

106 HEN CNER
306 HEN CNES

Name	(PLEASE PRINT)	
Address	Apt.#	
City	State/Prov.	Zip/Postal Code

* Terms and prices subject to change without notice. Sales tax applicable in N.Y.
** Canadian residents will be charged applicable provincial taxes and GST.
   All orders subject to approval. Offer limited to one per household.
   ® are registered trademarks of Harlequin Enterprises Limited.

PRES99   ©1998 Harlequin Enterprises Limited

HARLEQUIN PRESENTS®

Seduction
SWEET ~~REVENGE~~

They wanted to get even.
Instead they got...married!
by bestselling author

Penny Jordan

Don't miss Penny Jordan's latest enthralling miniseries
about four special women. Kelly, Anna, Beth and Dee
share a bond of friendship and a burning desire to
avenge a wrong. But in their quest for revenge, they
each discover an even stronger emotion.
Love.

Look out for all four books in Harlequin Presents®:

November 1999
THE MISTRESS ASSIGNMENT

December 1999
LOVER BY DECEPTION

January 2000
A TREACHEROUS SEDUCTION

February 2000
THE MARRIAGE RESOLUTION

Available at your favorite retail outlet.

HARLEQUIN®
Makes any time special ™

Look us up on-line at: http://www.romance.net   HPSRS

Don't miss a fabulous new trilogy
from a rising star in

HARLEQUIN ◆ PRESENTS®

KIM LAWRENCE

**Wanted:
three husbands
for three sisters!**

*Triplet sisters—they're
the best, the closest,
of friends…*

Meet lively, spirited Anna in
Wild and Willing!, Harlequin Presents® #2078
On sale December 1999

Lindy meets the man of her dreams in
The Secret Father, Harlequin Presents® #2096
On sale March 2000

Hope's story is the thrilling conclusion
to this fabulous trilogy in
An Innocent Affair, Harlequin Presents® #2114
On sale June 2000

Available wherever Harlequin books are sold.

◆ HARLEQUIN®
Makes any time special ™

Visit us at www.romance.net

HPTB1

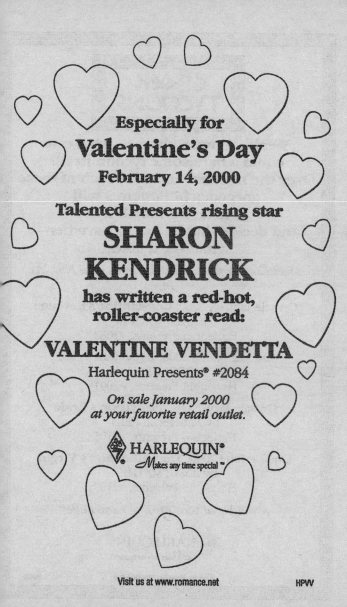

Especially for
Valentine's Day
February 14, 2000

Talented Presents rising star
SHARON KENDRICK
has written a red-hot,
roller-coaster read:

VALENTINE VENDETTA
Harlequin Presents® #2084

*On sale January 2000
at your favorite retail outlet.*

HARLEQUIN®
Makes any time special ™

Visit us at www.romance.net

HPVV

GREEK TYCOONS

Wealth, power, charm—what else could a handsome tycoon need? Over the next few months, each of these gorgeous billionaires will meet his match... and decide that he has to have her—whatever it takes!

Meet Constantine, Dio, Andreas and Nikolas in:

On sale January 2000: **Constantine's Revenge**
by KATE WALKER
Harlequin Presents, #2082

On sale March 2000: **Expectant Bride**
by LYNNE GRAHAM
Harlequin Presents, #2091

On sale May 2000: **The Tycoon's Bride**
by MICHELLE REID
Harlequin Presents, #2105

On sale June 2000: **The Millionaire's Virgin**
by ANNE MATHER
Harlequin Presents, #2109

Available at your favorite retail outlet.

HARLEQUIN®
Makes any time special ™

Visit us at www.romance.net

HPGT